A World Between

A World Between

Poems, Short Stories, and Essays
by Iranian-Americans

Edited by

PERSIS M. KARIM

and

MOHAMMAD MEHDI

KHORRAMI

George Braziller
NEW YORK

First published by George Braziller, Inc., in 1999

The copyright to each selection is held by its author.

For information, please address the publisher:
George Braziller, Inc.
171 Madison Avenue
New York, NY 10016

LIBRARY OF CONGRESS CATALOGING-IN-PUBLICATION DATA:
A world between : poems, short stories, and essays by Iranian Americans /
edited by Persis M. Karim and Mohammad Mehdi Khorrami.—1st ed.
    p. cm.
ISBN 0-8076-1445-9
1. American literature—Iranian American authors. 2. Iranian Americans—
Literary collections. 3. American literature—20th century.
4. Iranian Americans. I. Karim, Persis M. II. Khorrami, Mohammad Mehdi.
PS508.I69w67 1999
810.8'0989155—dc21   98-50369
                                        CIP

Designed by Neko Buildings

Printed and bound in the United States

First paperback edition

This book is dedicated to the people of Iran and the people of the United States—two nations that share a long history—with the hope that the future will witness dialogue and friendship between them.

Acknowledgments

The editors gratefully acknowledge the contributions of all the authors anthologized here. It is our hope that they continue to write and be read beyond this collection. We also thank the Center for Middle Eastern Studies at the University of Texas at Austin and M. R. "Moh" Ghanoonparvar for helping to bring some of these voices together in April 1998 at a conference of Iranian-American writers held in Austin, Texas. Zjaleh Hajibashi, Nika Khanjani, and Mary Harvan were invaluable for their suggestions, copyediting, and support. We are indebted to Mary Taveras at George Braziller, Inc., for guiding this project with sensitivity and intelligence. Lastly, we extend our thanks to Marjan Karim, who graciously lent her illustrative talents to this project under difficult time constraints.

Contents

⤐ Poems ⤐

>✎ *Short Stories* ✐

⋈ Essays ⋊

Foreword

Before the Iranian Revolution of 1979, when Iran and the United States were allies, Iranians came to the United States by and large as individuals for various reasons: to complete their education, to work, and some eventually to stay. For most, the break with the home country and its culture was neither definitive nor permanent. Back then one could continue living in both worlds, which, in many ways, seemed complementary. After the revolution, however, this situation changed dramatically. With the establishment of the Islamic Republic and the American hostage crisis, the two erstwhile allies became bitter enemies—a division that deepened during the Iran-Iraq War (1980–1988), when the United States tacitly sided with Iraq. During this first decade of hostility (which still continues), there occurred a major exodus of Iranians who were dissatisfied with conditions in their country. For the first time in modern history, there was an Iranian diaspora, the largest concentration of which settled on the North American Continent. For these émigrés and exiles and their offspring, there was little hope of or point in returning; nor was there a full adjustment to their adopted homeland, where they were commonly regarded with animosity.

This is the plight out of which most of the contributors to this collection present their experiences and findings. Most write in the first person, and most are women. Not all, however, are, in the words of one writer, "children of the revolution." Some left Iran earlier. Nevertheless, for these authors the revolution and its aftermath constitute the momentous turning point in their lives, resulting in their displacement.

These voices, as such, are distinctive for their transitional or "transnational" duality. All here are identifiably Iranian in having Persian as their language of heritage (although some are more comfortable with Persian than others), yet also Western in expressing themselves in English. Beyond language, however, is the deeper pull of their transitional experience and memory, which are entirely Iranian. Hence, the reader is presented with a split, not a fusion. Nowhere is there registered a hope that in forgetting or in setting aside a remembered past there will be a harmonious integration between the polarized aspects of one's existence and identity. The cure for these writers is not to leave one culture behind and merge into another, but rather to tell their stories and to acknowledge their dividedness.

This is the message that one comes away with: where there is blending, there is difference. Those who see that from their own experience and turn to writing contribute, in the process, to the record of a still unclosed chapter of human history. As one writer states, "I mourn my past." The language is English, but the memory and its pain are Iranian.

DONNÉ RAFFAT

Preface

On the day of my dissertation defense at the University of Texas at Austin several years ago, the members of my committee asked me why I had chosen the subject of exile and its influence on the life and writings of Victor Hugo, a prominent nineteenth-century French author, as my topic. Although I had prepared extensive notes on the subject, I involuntarily answered: "Because I am a writer in exile and I think I can recount my life story through this dissertation." I had no intention of continuing beyond this, but my advisor insisted that I elaborate. I began to tell them the story of my life: the way I had left Iran, my wanderings in unknown countries, the numerous jobs I had taken to survive, my efforts to find a new home. I remember little of the exact details of that day, other than the surprised looks on the faces of my committee members. I do, however, remember the last sentence of my opening comments. "You know," I said, "the life of an exile is short. It begins with his escape from his home country and it ends with his death in the host country. After his death there's no reminder of his existence. So, recounting his story, even if through a dissertation, is the least an exile ought to be allowed to do."

Indeed, I believed this would be the fullest expression of my experiences as an exile until one of my many conversations with Persis Karim, a friend and colleague, who suggested the idea for this book. I thought about the kinds of experiences that my second generation friends would write about. I tried to imagine their stories. It soon became clear to me that their stories resemble many of the stories of exiles, communicating a sense of alienation, of being an outsider, and a feeling of in-betweenness. This similarity convinced me that what exiles and immigrants carry with them is often passed on to the next generation. For me, this book is a literary translation of those scars and of the efforts of many of its authors to feel whole again by acknowledging the disparate parts of their existence.

MOHAMMAD MEHDI KHORRAMI

In the spring of 1990, I attended a panel discussion at a conference that concerned Iranian immigration to the United States after the revolution and the adjustment problems of expatriates and exiles in Los Angeles. I listened to three panelists (two sociologists and one anthropologist) who described the difficult psychological, emotional, and economic transitions that these immigrants were undergoing in the face of tremendous anti-Iranian feeling in this country. At the end of the session, I raised my hand and asked the anthropologist about the children of these immigrants and the difficulties they faced in trying to bridge these two cultures. The woman seemed unfazed by my question. "Those who were born here or who came here as children don't have any such problems. They speak the language comfortably, they live in American society, they have no difficulties per se." I was flabbergasted by her response since much of my childhood had been devoted to explaining what kind of name I had, why I ate lamb instead of hamburgers, and rice instead of potatoes. I knew I was different. It was only because of the revolution and the sudden influx of Iranians that I could find any vocabulary for who and what I was.

After the panel was dismissed, two young women approached me and thanked me for my question. Both of them were annoyed by the panelist's answer. They, too, were half Iranian (one woman had an American mother and an Iranian father, while the other had an Iranian father and an Italian mother). Like me, they had been looking for a way to articulate their experience of being part Iranian and part American. We joked then that we were "half-breeds" and that despite our deficiency at speaking Persian, we, too, were part of the spectrum of Iranian-Americans in this country who had grown up in the shadow of the Iranian Revolution and the hostage crisis. When I finally learned the Persian word for people like me, *do-rageh* ("two veined"), with two bloods running through me, I began to embrace my complex heritage and to see that it enriched me. This book is for those young people who, like me, have searched for ways to express and understand the complexities of what it means to live in the aftermath of their parents' migrations.

PERSIS M. KARIM

Introduction

During a conference of Iranian-American writers held in Austin, Texas, we heard Arash Saedinia, one of the writers in this collection, describe himself as "intensely Iranian-American—that is to say, I am neither Iranian nor American." *A World Between: Poems, Short Stories, and Essays by Iranian-Americans* was born from that experience of in-betweenness shared by Saedinia, ourselves, and the many other writers represented here. As the first published collection of original writing by Iranian-Americans, this book offers a glimpse into the lives of an American ethnic group often understood only stereotypically through the prism of the 1979 Iranian Revolution and U.S.-Iranian political relations over the past two decades.

The Iranian Revolution, which overthrew the Shah in February 1979, left the Iranian nation in great political turmoil. Before the end of the year, it emerged as the Islamic Republic of Iran. Ayatollah Ruhollah Khomeini, who had been living in exile first in Iraq and later in France, returned to Iran to take up the spiritual and political leadership of the nation. In November 1979, a group of armed students occupied the U.S. embassy in Tehran and took fifty-two people hostage. The ensuing hostage crisis—one of the most publicized political events in U.S. history—had a lasting effect on Iran's standing in the international community and on U.S. policies toward Iran in the following decades. In fact, media coverage of the events of 1979–1980 has been instrumental in shaping American attitudes toward Iran, the Iranian people, and the Middle East generally. Many Iranian-Americans have often felt concerned, ambivalent, and at times even ashamed about revealing their heritage in an atmosphere steeped with media images portraying Iranians as hostile, as fanatical, and above all as terrorists during the period of the revolution, the Iran-Iraq War, and as recently as the 1991 conflict known as the Persian Gulf War.

The dramatic social upheaval following the Iranian Revolution produced one of the largest mass migrations in recent history. From 1979 until the mid-1980s, more than 3 million Iranians emigrated to Europe and North America. Often thought of as a homogeneous culture—one aspect of the inaccurate image Americans have of Iranians—Iran, in fact, enjoys a diverse national culture. Iranians are a religiously and ethnically mixed population. Although the dominant religious group is Shi'i Muslim, Iranians in and outside of Iran belong to the Zoroastrian, Jewish, Baha'i, and Christian faiths. Similarly, while the dominant language group in Iran is Persian speaking (known in Iran by its indigenous name "Farsi"), other major ethnic groups include Kurds, Azerbaijanis, Turks, Armenians, Assyrians, and Arabs. In addition to ethnic and religious differences, Iranians in North America are of varying socioeconomic and political backgrounds. This collection reflects some of these diverse influences. It also addresses the many effects of the revolution on Iranian-Americans, twenty years after that historic event.

Of those Iranians who emigrated to Europe and North America, more than 1 million came to the United States. Many sought relief from political and religious persecution. Others sought to escape the effects of the Iran-Iraq War, which erupted in 1980, and the difficult economic conditions that accompanied the eight-year conflict. Many Iranians intended to leave only temporarily, although it soon became clear that some would risk prison or death were they to return. Many who had fundamental differences with the new government of the Islamic Republic of Iran chose not to return. Twenty years after the revolution, many of these exiles, refugees, and immigrants have become permanent residents and citizens of the United States. Iranian-American communities have burgeoned in California (Los Angeles, which has the largest population of Iranians, is often called "Tehrangeles"), New York, Texas, Illinois, Maryland, and Washington, D.C.

If the Iranian Revolution led to the expansion of the Iranian-American population in the United States, it also galvanized them as a community and marked them in the public eye. Not only new immigrants, but all Iranian-Americans were affected by the revolution, by the strained U.S.-Iranian political relations that followed, and by derogatory media representations of Iranians—and Middle Easterners in general—as terrorists and religious fundamentalists. Iranians have been targeted for denials of visas, for unnecessary background checks, and for airport searches, and along with Arabs during the Persian Gulf War, they were lumped together as the enemy of the West. The revolution and U.S.-Iranian politics have also separated families by restricting movement between the two nations, a painful example of how governments and their policies can wreak havoc on the everyday lives of their citizens.

While we have chosen to utilize a standard generic organization for this anthology (poems, short stories, and essays), we recognize how common themes surface in all three genres. We have attempted to offer a range of voices, experiences, and sentiments in the selections by authors who represent first- and second-generation Iranian-Americans, as well as those whose proximity and relationship to the country of Iran may be more distant.

Some of the stories and poems emerge from the experiences of Iranians who consider themselves exiles and whose families would have been at risk had they remained in Iran after the revolution. Those who have been affected by political exile and whose families are scattered across the globe, find a voice in poems like those of Laleh Khalili, Zara Houshmand, and Sanaz Nikaein. "My Father's Shoes," a poem by fourteen-year-old Solmaz Sharif, conveys the pain of exile through the poignant image of the shoes her father wore when he last stood on Iranian soil. Another kind of exile, which could be characterized

23

as spiritual exile, is expressed in poems by Ali Zarrin and the essay "Pregnant with Sorrow" by Nasrin Rahimieh. Their work addresses the separation from home, country, and family and the longing for that lost connection that was further severed by the revolution and the difficulties of maintaining ties to their families in Iran after 1979. The political, cultural, and emotional fallout from the revolution has touched most Iranian families, whether they were displaced by the revolution or they migrated at different historical moments. Some authors, including Nasrin Rahimieh, Nahid Rachlin, and Zjaleh Hajibashi, represent individual and prerevolutionary migrations and multicultural unions between Iranians and other nationalities. Their works reflect dualistic perspectives—an awareness of both Iran and North America and of what it means to be "in between."

This collection also bridges that first generation of Iranian immigrants who were born and raised in Iran and who recall the period prior to the revolution, as well as those younger Iranian-Americans who were born in the United States and consider themselves to be both Iranian and American. Our deliberate use of the hyphen in "Iranian-American" is meant to represent this synthesis of two distinct cultures. We also use it to suggest the state of in-betweeness many Iranian-Americans find themselves in, as well as the process by which Iranians living in America have begun to claim their ethnicity as Americans.

Much of the writing by first-generation Iranian-Americans draws on childhood memories of Iran and on the images, colors, and textures that resonate with Iranians wherever they are. The second generation of Iranian-Americans—born of immigrants either in Iran or the United States but raised largely in the West—is now reaching adulthood and attending universities. Exposed to Iranian culture and the Persian language to varying degrees, this generation has a more tenuous connection with Iran, having grown up in the shadow of the hostage crisis and the political tensions between the United States and Iran. Tara Fatemi's poems about her Iranian identity highlight the difficulties of claiming that identity in the context of such a culture. She and others have struggled to come to terms with their identity as Iranian-Americans, influenced not only by U.S. attitudes toward Iran but also by Iranian immigrants anxious to preserve their culture and language within a nation often hostile to them and their homeland.

Although some of the authors were born in the United States or immigrated during their childhood, many retain strong links to Iranian culture through their parents and grandparents, who continue to struggle with the English language and cultural assimilation. These authors recognize the importance of maintaining some continuity with their family's past and of nurturing a relationship with Iranian culture. Arash Saedinia's poems about his grandparents evoke the old world in which they lived—images that link him to Iran, a place he hasn't seen since he was a small child. The tension of belonging to both—and neither—Iranian and U.S. cultures arises in many of the collection's works. Nika Khanjani's "The Eyebrow" and Persis M. Karim's poem "Hybrid" point to the particular expectations of those growing up female in Iranian culture. Several pieces address the experience of having mixed Iranian and American parentage. Nahid Rachlin's "Search" recounts one Iranian-American woman's search for her mother in Iran after a failed marriage with an American man. The theme of growing up Iranian-American when it was often easier to deny that heritage is found in other works. One example is Mariam Salari's "Ed McMahon Is Iranian." Growing up in the United States with unusual and perhaps difficult-to-pronounce names, or having dark skin, dark eyes, and noticeably pronounced features, have impressed many of these young writers with a sense both of their own difference and of the urgency of finding a voice when it would have been easier to remain silent. The essay by Fereydoun Safizadeh, "Children of the Revolution," addresses some of the difficulties the second generation faces and how they have struggled to claim their

Iranian identity and at the same time minimize the pain of this identification. Many of the poems and stories articulate the complex and difficult feelings attached to being Iranian in the United States because of the many powerful, enduring images and stereotypes of Iranians generated by U.S. television, film, and media coverage of political events. Although this collection is not a definitive representation of all Iranian-Americans (either politically or culturally), it does give voice to an emerging American ethnic group that has often been unable to speak for itself.

The works in this collection also show how Iranian culture pervades the food, language, and gestures of everyday life of Iranian-Americans. Persian proverbs and expressions, which are sprinkled throughout conversations in Iranian-American households, surface in these poems and stories. Many of the writers use Persian words, some providing their own definitions and footnotes. As editors, we have chosen not to include a glossary of Persian words because, frequently, repetition or other images adequately convey the desired meanings. Furthermore, we thought it was important for readers, regardless of their heritage, to encounter language as Iranian-Americans hear and speak it. In the mixing of cultures, languages take on new meanings, new dynamics. Hidden within them are traces of migrations, travels, and exilic wandering. Laleh Khalili's poem "In Exile," for instance, uses the word *azizam* without translating it. The word means "my dear," but by not translating it into English, the speaker dramatically conveys her message addressed to her native country. Similarly, Maryam Ovissi provides no translation in her poem, "Khorshid." The Persian word for "sun," *khorshid* has resonance both in the significance of the image and in the sound of the word when pronounced by an English speaker. Arash Saedinia's poems also highlight the importance of the Persian language in his relationship with his grandparents. Some words like *ta'rof*, which appear in many of the pieces in this collection, simply cannot be translated into English. Images

26

of pomegranates, goldfish, *nowruz* (the Persian New Year that begins on the vernal equinox and celebrates the arrival of spring) and its customs and rituals, and Persian cuisine, are a distinct part of the landscape of this culture and its continuation on this continent.

Several authors have recently traveled to Iran, either for the first time or after a long separation, only to discover that they can no more be completely Iranian than they can be completely American. Distance from Iran has often created an idealized image of the homeland. Many of these works bear traces of such an idealization of Persian traditions, customs, cuisine, landscape, and family relationships. Some of the authors portray the disillusion of discovering that warm family relationships can also grow tiresome, as in Roxanne Varzi's "The Pelican." As Firoozeh Kashani-Sabet's "Martyrdom Street" suggests, Iran, no different from any other place, can also be intolerably depressing.

Some of the work in this collection is not directly focused on Iran or on being Iranian-American. Allowing this literature to move beyond a set of standardized images, forms, or expectations is important to developing any national or ethnic literary voice. This volume provides a forum for many Iranian-American authors, regardless of whether or not their work has distinct Iranian references. Yet the influences of migration and the history of the last twenty years are always present. For many authors, giving voice to Iranian-American themes and issues is of central importance. But like all communities and ethnic groups, Iranian-Americans don't want to be caught in the never-ending spiral of old images that tie them to the homeland. Rather, these authors point to their syncretic, evolving, and dualistic experiences as writers, thinkers, and citizens who perhaps live in "a world between."

PERSIS M. KARIM

MOHAMMAD MEHDI KHORRAMI

A World Between

❀ Poems ❀

ARASH SAEDINIA

*namaz**

empty pickle jars line
the bottom of the pantry
gossiping in vinegar.
they await the alchemist's blessing
eager to join the consecrated
vessels amassed above
flush with tarragon and mint
saffron and thyme.
the cupboard is a shrine
each tea tin a reliquary
every burlap rice sack a benediction.

"try this," you murmured
and laughed as I puzzled over
the red leather bulb
a fat sunburned king
with a tiny stem crown.
it was my first pomegranate.
at ten I made *chai***
you let me
praised me for it
though I was always the guest
always will be.

---

* The prayer Muslims perform five times a day.
** Persian for tea.

twenty thousand
casserole afternoons
a lifetime of prayer
forever on your knees
crushing lentils into paste
drying herbs on bronze platters
pressing forehead to floor
have turned your spine into limestone
and you still start from scratch
one eye on the sun
the other on me
addasi, ash reshteh, ghormeh sabzi***
I have tasted your love songs.

***These are all traditional Persian dishes.

nowruz*

"goldfish are cheap,
dollar a dozen.
wait'll you see the rest."
I pointed to sea horses, angel fish, porcupine puffers,
"goldfish," grandma whispered, "two of them."

the shopkeeper fetched her a pair of aces,
they danced in the bowl like ochre bullion,
flashed like canary ducats. *Carassius auratus.*
the kind you'd expect in a picture
by the dictionary definition.

two weeks into the new year,
her nightstand bare.
"*naneh* . . . the goldfish?"
"they had nothing to eat," she mumbled,
frowning to keep from crying.
"no one to feed them."

---

* *Nowruz*, literally "new day," refers to the Iranian New Year and marks the arrival of
spring. Goldfish, among other things, serve as symbols of good fortune and are tra-
ditionally found in Iranian households during New Year celebrations.

*dastet dard nakoneh**

grandma can't thread
a needle anymore,
says, "it's better I die"
as though it will happen
soon. until then,
I'll thread her needles.

---

* A Persian expression of thanks whose rough translation is "May your hand be free of pain."

yeki bud, yeki nabud*

what goes without saying?
ours is a history of silence,
an assemblage of garments
strung on a clothesline of
glyph glances and idle chatter.

my tongue, built of porcelain,
dams a decade of questions,
moots that have faded
like the cerulean marks
on your fingers and forehead.

I carry your image
in the book that you gave me,
sewn from your lips.
the story begins:
one was, one wasn't.

---

* Literally, "one was, one wasn't." It is the Persian equivalent of "once upon a time."

*ta'rof**

I.

she's there again,
pouring tea leaves
onto the dew-soaked lawn,
scattering rice scraps beneath
the weeping willow.
sparrows converge,
as always.

II.

"during shortfalls, your
grandmother would fast for days,
place her portion on our plates.
each time she'd insist,
'I have eaten.'"

III.

sure as the dawn,
her first words are, *"ghaza khordi?"*

---

* Having no English equivalent, *ta'rof* refers to the intricate rituals of giving and receiving between host and guest in Iranian culture.

38

"have you eaten?"
as I mumble, "I have,"
naneh turns toward the kitchen
and replies, "eat again love,
eat again."

shab bekher*

I have her hair
thick, jet, indelicate
a hint of my inheritance:
the furrows and marks implied
by flesh, hidden in the frame,
seducing gravity.

she sleeps on her back
hair in braids,
talks in sleep.
I lie on my side,
rooms apart,
and listen with my marrow
for fragments
of her speech.

---

*The equivalent of "good night," *shab bekher* literally means "night to rest" or "ease."

*donya hamineh**

grandpa's been old all my life
older than this forsaken century
ageless as the ruins of Persia.
here, in the tenth decade, *Haj Agha's***
begun his infirmity, tied to a catheter
and a small room with a bed.

"this is the world,"
grandma sighs, folding and unfolding
the kerchief in her lap.

grandpa calls her *naneh* now,
and mother she has been,
matriarch of dozens,
fast as the columns of Persepolis
that endure to bear the
weight.

---

* The literal translation of this Persian phrase is "This is the world." It is similar to "the way it is" in English.
** *Haj Agha* is a title of respect bestowed upon devout older men who have made the pilgrimage to Mecca. The title for a woman is *Haj Khanum*.

cheshmetun rowshan*

his kisses have grown weaker
though no less honest.
I bend my head that he might
hold my chin and
purse his wizened lips
against both cheeks.
each time I
draw myself away
his hand lingers
in the space between us
as though cast
in a lost song of praise.

there's still strength
in his gaze
though cataracts have patched
a pall over the amber of his eyes.
muggish and musty
his irises gloss
like dust ridden gilt
in the window of a storefront
shrouded by sunset.
beneath the ether of age

---

* A congratulatory phrase that translates, "May your eyes be bright."

and a haze of senescence
lie embers of amber.

grandma tries his flitting mind
grips my wrist and murmurs,
"Kiyeh?"
"Who is he?"
grandpa rustles, mouths my name.
"Arasheh."
grandma beams, leans toward him,
asks, "Khoshetun miyad?"
"Does he please you?"
grandpa pauses, turns and replies,
"Nureh-cheshameh."
"He's the light of my eyes."

takhteh-nard*

my grandfather taught me the physics of chance
in the TACK T-TAck Tack of dice against teak.
grandpa indulged my stammering fingers,
warbling hints between sips of tea.

rhythm and math congealed in the sixes of
ivories and triangle spaces, as I learned each roll's
name and scheme: *"panj-o-seh"*
*"chahar-o-do" "shish-o-yek" "joft panj."***

I never won a full hand. too young, too rough on
the toss. too busy watching *Haj Agha*.

---

* Persian for "backgammon."
** *Yek, do, seh, chahar, panj,* and *shish* are Persian for numbers "one" through "six." *Joft*
means "double."

piri bad ast*

my grandfather's feet are swollen from sitting
his calves have grown soft and bruise without effort.

"Haj Agha," I squawk, "yeh sher bekhun barayeh ma."
"give us a poem."

seance of sense, grandpa's hand charts the tract
between brow and chin. his fingers map the mind's aisles

as Ferdowsi and Hafez** haunt the shelf-worn passages,
rustling the palsied sheets scattered on the floor.

naneh buzzes, "piri bad ast" and advises me against it
while grandpa cloaks his mouth and coughs

to mask the sound
of his tearing breath.

---

* Literally, "old age is bad."
** Two of the most renowned authors of classical Persian poetry.

My Turn

third grade recess
we sit in the playground
a circle of girls
one by one:

*I'm one half German one
quarter French one quarter Dutch
I'm one quarter Swiss one quarter
Belgian one half Italian one half*
so many fractions I crave
pieces of beautiful European cultures
the ones we learn about in school
details drilled into our minds

*I'm one half American
one half Persian*
a girl scowls
*both your parents are from
over there
aren't they?*
I stammer *but I was born here*
she rolls her eyes
*You're not half American
you are one hundred percent
I-rain-e-an*

I dig chin into chest
clench leg muscles tight
so I won't run.

I Ain't No American Beauty Rose

dirty
brown
ugly
weed
I am
responsible
for American
hostages
ten years
I cultivate
courage
to be myself
plant seeds
for pride
in heritage
man cackles
Shave your eyebrows
fuckin'
A-rab!
thick eyebrows
of my mother
grandmother
I want to pluck
all ancestry
his scythed
tongue
bleeds me.

TARA FATEMI

Five P.M. Express

drunk man
stumbles onto train
features and coloring my own

heads shake in disapproval
train conductor collects tickets
tells man the fare
(one dollar more than at station)
he grunts, mumbles words I barely recognize
as *Farsi*
hands conductor one dollar too little

conductor's face reddens, wrinkles
this pathetic drunk man who
can't even speak English

a couple people try to pay
the missing fare
conductor refuses
I'm letting you go this time
next time I see you
you better have that extra dollar!

one passenger yells
go back to I-ran or I-raq, stupid
Iranian smiles at me
I remember magazine covers

Melting pot boils over
Poll results:
Majority of Americans are
against immigrants
I slide lower in my seat
remember women on the bus
all those foreigners coming over
how can our kids learn anything in school?

I glance over he is
still smiling and looking oh God
he can't mistake me for a friend
blow my cover
everyone will point their fingers
laugh at me too until
we are so far beneath them we are
not part of their world

but I am invisible already
I cannot see who I am
only who I am not.

My Fifties-Theme Birthday Party

I'll be the coolest girl there
envy of all the ten-year-olds
tougher than Pinky Tuscadero
I'll have everything but the motorcycle

my mother offers to sew a poodle
onto a skirt
I imagine other girls with authentic clothes
their moms had worn as kids
my mother, so thrilled by her creation
I pity her
she was never a teenager
in America

at the party we listen
to borrowed tapes of Elvis
and Chuck Berry
I wear jeans
an old white work shirt
and red eyes
my mother was born
in the wrong country

ten years later
my mother throws away old clothes
I pull an Iranian housedress from the pile
my mother laughs as I

gush over the rich colors and intricate beads
it's tacky, you don't want it
I rub the fabric and see a seamstress in Iran
sewing each bead with care, with precision
an old beautiful woman
perhaps an ancestor
a sharer of blood

I imagine my mother
wearing this dress in Iran
her home I've seen only once
when I refused to learn *Farsi*
I disappointed all my relatives

Now I look at my mother
and feel my Persian blood
flow proud
her gift to me

you'll never wear that thing,
just throw it away!
but I wear the dress
that I have rescued
it has rescued me.

Disassociation

1.

We are not precise people
We are not precise people

We measure our duration by ambiguous clocks
and count our blessings in forgotten numerologies

Our memories have decayed
through
the collective alchemy of our enemies' memories
and
our own daily drowning
daily drowning

2.

"I remember You stepping out of Yourself
I remember You naked but for the profusion
of shit, sweat, and blood
I remember You in Your mute frenetic movements
asserting the validity of Your existence

When did I abandon You?
Through which cycles of moon

which cycles of birth
did I abandon You?

Beloved, when did I forget that beyond the corruption of Your wounds,
I had loved You once vigorously
When did I forget that Your hands disfigured by the leprosy of despair
had known me once
in the intimate manner of mothers or forbidden lovers?
Beloved, when did I abandon You?"

3.

We define the boundaries of Our souls
by the accepted notions of
Our image in the public looking glass of another's society

We are a lonely people
desperate for the acceptance of Our ambiguous superiority
desperate for the acknowledgment of Our historic accomplishments
this vast landscape of ruin and silence

We adopt the language of Our conquerors
and assimilate Our hangman's history

We break bread with Our enemies and
invite them to burn Our house down
while we drink wine and hemlock
and seduce their warriors in sordid beds of betrayal

We are bastards of a thousand nations,
not precise in remembering our memories

4.

"I am not as I was
I am not as I will be
I am not as You want me

I am not a declaration of possibilities
nor evidence of universality

I am that ephemeral moment in history
when truth and reality fornicate
in a cruel sandstorm of birth and destruction

strip me bare and honest
strip me bare
I,
the mutant progenitor of millenniums of war

I bear, still, after so many silences,
the stigmata of Your love
I carry the wounds of Your transgression in my womb
and the memory of your destruction in the unconscious growth of
electricity in my limbs

I am not as You remember me
I am not I as I remember You
I now speak the language of Your rape"

Why the hell American Revolutionaries bother the hell out of me . . .

I didn't have the luxury of not being exotic
and I didn't look for danger
because in my blood
fear flowed
and I forgot words
as mothers betrayed their sons
and brothers raped their sisters

I didn't have the simple choice of disagreement
and the airwaves didn't belong to me
and in my country
      words were instruments of torture

I learned that
every syllable was a code
and I spoke in tongues
unfamiliar to strangers
and my enemies
watched my house
and watched my legs as they
carried me street to house
      to street
and watched the motion of my jaws
lest I reclaim my mother tongue

I didn't have the luxury of finding
war the subject of protest
as it bulldozed my shelter
and revolution wasn't the symbol of rebellion of adolescents in
the throes of proving their manhood

instead
I washed my hands
in my sisters' blood and
tried to feel the pulse of hope in
their collar bones
instead I learned semiautomatic weapons' caress on my palms
for the phallic gestures of a patriarchy
obsessed with its pissing ability were not foreign to me.

I didn't know anything about speech
as the primitive right to
name objects
had become a subversive
activity

I didn't have the luxury of not being exotic

I didn't . . .

I learned to understand the hands of
strangers in my underwear
drawers searching
for words

I learned to understand the
pragmatic rules which govern the gravity of friendship

I learned to appreciate that the walls
which kept me in
kept the world out

I didn't have the luxury of polemic
in my land and the simple act of
remembering memories
was treasonous . . .

And organization?
Pah!
We prided ourselves in paranoia
for no one can be honest in a land
where a refrigerator and a
matinee admission to heaven
buy your
progenies' lives,
buy your ancestors' history,
buy your honor
and your damn soul too . . .

And I awake every morning
and I breathe
and I speak
and I speak
and I read
and I read
and I lay possession to words and images and sounds obsessively:
they say one craves what one was denied in childhood . . .

Defeated

At Home

Forsaken by a century hurtling by,
we slowly unlearned our ancestry
in search of a definition in solidarity with the remainder of the
    universe:

smuggled videos and bootlegged foreign music
satellite dishes hawking naked flesh
diluted *farangi** perfume and fake *farangi* clothes
broken *farangi* tongues and adapted *farangi* wives
black-market *farangi* appliances even:
these irrefutable symbols of legitimacy and progress

On the other hand,
our history devoured us with the final fervor of
an insatiable ghoul who sees her lifeline fraying at the ends

We lost ourselves.
We lost ourselves.
And the darkness that claimed us forcefully to a prior incarnation
did not emanate from the womb which had shouted us in amniotic
    ecstasy

---

* Persian for "foreign."

We are not entirely about salvation
nor about fattened prosperity
Our numbers defy a singular notion of passion and desire

Obsessed with the unique superiority of our race
we have survived so long
we have survived so hard
that shape-shifting is coded into our marrow and our memory

In Exile

Azizam, shamefaced I am, just shamefaced.

The other day, you know,
I denied being yours
I denied being you
I denied it all

the other day,
I had to learn to unlearn you
the other day

Azizam, how does one recount a story
in a language no one seems to understand?

There are times when you want to be a profusion of myths
when you know that
dormant histories lie unassumingly in the forgotten subcutaneous
    region of your rib cage
There are times that you JUST want to declare yourself
in joy
in joy
in pride, even
and you can't

the Esperanto of screaming or laughter or sorrow or rage, raising
    of eyebrows,
or lowering of eyelids

all have different meanings here,
and you know that you will be misconstrued
and you know that you will be misunderstood
and you know that you will be ridiculed.

Azizam, what can one do when
one protects the fragile genealogy of an entire history?
What can one do?
Shamefaced I am, *azizam*, just shamefaced.

MARYAM OVISSI

Untitled

My fall has arrived.

The leaves from my tree have begun to fall
and now I have a sweet-scented tea
that I have yet to taste.

The end of my infancy is present
and soon my adolescence will begin.

The water is waiting to change from a simmer to a boil
and not until the water is able to release its heat
may my tea seep in the pot.

I look forward to tasting the fruits of my farmer's labor.

Above all, I hope the tea will be both bitter and sweet.

In Iran, the duality of taste is accepted by the palette
with the placement of a sweet cube.

I look forward to smelling the tea's scent
rising and carrying the memories of my past
as well as serving as my guide into the future.

Khorshid

The ground is still cold from last month's storm.

I walk each day and each day the earth hardens beneath my step.

With my promenade, I create new mounds and valleys
unintentionally, but merely as a ramification of apathy.

Fecund darkness precariously spreads its wings into my world
and there, I await the simplicity of the *khorshid*.

There, I am and there is no depth to my being.

The *khorshid* shows her face with bravery today
and the ground swells to her calling.

On the Way to the Caucasus
(Crossing the Delijan Pass)

It struck like lightning.
May I be made stone-still if I lie.

Then I began consuming whole loaves of bread.
The entire week's cheese ration
and green plums straight from the tree.

Suddenly my travels stopped.
May I be immobile like the mountain peaks
if I lie.

The purple earth betrayed its will
to remain still.
Under the cover of darkness,
all the ash trees fled the village
and the clouds changed into waves,
rocking me sick.

I had been mystified
by the gem-like glow of his cigarette tip
and the whisper of the two-string *tar*
on a night of heat and opium smoke.

Suddenly my travels stopped on the way to the Caucasus.
May I remain forever in the mud of Bessarabia,
May I never become myself again if I lie.

The Secret Alley

I know a forgotten alley that will lead you
to the hanging gardens of Babylon
where water and earth will be offered to you
and you will tread on the soil
where Cyrus and Darius lingered
on the muddy banks of the Euphrates
to gaze at the first moon
and contemplate the stars
smelling the fresh mint wild in the air.

I cannot tell you much about Sumer and Akkad
but one thing is clear.
There, too, men were awed
at the sight of the glittering spears
the nearing thunder of hooves and drums,
the golden dust cloud raised by the immortals,
and women barely managed
to stop the carafes of hair-thin glass
from shattering into a thousand colored pieces.

Darya Poshteh
(an all-female sea resort)

Oh! the racket of these crickets
in the gardenia plants,
and the walnuts falling,
falling one by one on the yellow tin-roof.

The sea gray-green mud.
The beach drowning slowly,
disappearing toward the invading Volga.
A floating curtain
halves the sea by gender.

Our galoshes bird beaks
drifting on the foaming waves.
Ourselves colored balloons
sinking down heavy,
trapped in yards of chintz.

Oh the blue sky!
What times! Wouldn't you know?

Knowing about War

I gather all my things.
How the calm shadows of old cypresses in the yard
no longer arrest my glance,
no longer hold my step captive in their cool assurance.
The fold of the curtains
and their years of loyalty fail me.
I see through their finely woven schemes,
a boy running down the alley
without a shoe.
A donkey abandons his load of tomatoes
in the desolate square,
his eyes crazed with fear
he circles the half-empty pool.
There is war outside.
I gather all my things
and sit waiting.

The World

Nothing fools you,
not even the sight of the hibiscus
under the snow or grandfather happily
chewing on coffee beans
after an afternoon out,
on a momentous errand.

You play the mandolin
and prune the cherry tree,
knowing all along that
the world is not round as you are told,
but that it is a long, rope-thin line,
stretching to eternity,
which is just around the corner anyhow.

The Year of the Winds

By the rosemary field
where the sun always sets
dyeing the world purple.
Is that where we met?
Was it not the year of the winds?

In Tabas, there were signs everywhere,
when the sycamores refused to bloom,
when aunty cured her aching back
with dried bread dipped in yolk,
and the winds filled the pots and pans
with powdery sand.

Who was it that kissed Robabeh
making her cheeks scarlet
and her belly a watermelon?

Had we traveled all that way to Tabas
or did we grow up there
by the fallen ramparts of dried mud and hay?

Was it in Tabas that we met
or another town we cannot remember?

I Pass

You deal, the wide world.
I hold the cards close to my chest;
I bluff.
You call.
I pass.

In a crowd,
in a mall,
in a mob,
I pass.

"You speak English very well."
Damn right, and so do you.
This language is my meat,
my trade, my life's blood,
my weapon and my drug of choice.
I'd slice you open with it,
but I pass.

"Zara. What a pretty name.
Where's it from?"
The far side of the moon,
I pass.

Zaragosa, Zarazuela, Zarathustra, Zara Dada.
But, God forbid, not Zahra.
Don't strangle me, don't bury me alive.

Beneath the veil
you find the bearded lady.
If you want to look,
you pay.

An acting exercise:
strange,
huddled in this private place
I say my name, again, again, again.
Zara . . . Zara . . . Zara . . .
So strange this name,
so strange
how my name
brings tears into my eyes.
And in my voice I hear:
a knife,
dead lovers calling me,
a voice beyond the grave
deep, deep inside;
a child unheard for many years
and still she hasn't grown.
Zara, innocent,
welcome,
home.

Exile, 1

Stepping out in the L.A. day,
like quilts spread out to an alien sun,
you make me a gift of this route, the way
it speaks to you; you offer, one by one:
a public path worn private, a tunnel,
the view through a flower's eye, points in space
where forgotten smells, discovered, funnel
an emptiness into the heart, a place
still hollow for another place, still raw
to the routes of escape. Above, a crow
hawks rumors; below the blades of grass claw,
grasping, at the sidewalk cracks. Still, they grow,
recalling birches shimmering like hope
in the creases of a far mountain slope.

Exile, 2

They say that this is as far as you go,
here, where the sound of the waves
bounces back off the cliffs
and returns on itself,
white noise washing and washing again
the blood from out of our voices.

They say that this is the end of the road:
an ocean, an ocean of waiting;
with waves to lick your open wounds,
with salt that bites,
with salt that leaches
the color from out of the blood.

Beached, what difference an angel, a ghost,
in this vast and narrow place?
I see driftwood in your face,
and waste, an ocean of waste,
in these bleached and twisted cords,
these dry veins rooted on another shore.

Transit Lounge

Window cleaners on scaffolding
climb the thin glass skin
scuttling muffled across the
               (limbo dance
               out of step
               with the Muzak inside)
incandescent blue beyond
the international grid;
intensely blue until
the long arm of the squeegee
cuts a diamond gash
and shows the jet-fume grime for what it is.

Rubberoid hours rebound in this purgatory;
the board flips ETAs, delays,
simultaneous translation
of two cities superimposed,
miles and miles of grilled earth
where the Alborz butts L.A.

Eid Nowruz *in Seattle*

Set on the table,
seven Ss
to symbolize *Eid Nowruz*,
Persian New Year:
Sir, Sekkeh, Sumaqh,
Sib, Shirini, Sabzi, Serkeh
garlic, gold coins, sumac,
apples, sweetmeats, sprouted wheat, vinegar.
My aunt completes the *sofreh*
with a silver-framed mirror, goldfish in a bowl,
hyacinths and an old Qu'ran.

The first day of spring,
the first day of the year.
I ran in the morning,
cedar trail fragrant with rain.
The sun peeped through the persistent clouds;
another day of hide-and-seek.

Red tulips I planted in winter
shoot up outside the window.
The yard is a colorful spring story
waiting to be told.

We sit at the table
after calling our family in Tehran,
voices echoing over the poor connection.

For lunch:
rice made with green herbs,
white fish seasoned with saffron,
and red tea in clear glasses.
My aunt, two cousins and me,
silent,
but for clinking forks
and Iranian pop music.

The Sound of Home

Lately
I have been trying to remember
the sound of the waves near my home.
All I hear are the gurgling creeks
winding through this rolling Hill Country
once submerged under an ocean
now thick with red cedar and live oak.
The waves invisible now,
I cup my hands over my ears
and try to listen to the echo of this ancient sea.
All I hear is the Arabian Sea sighing for my return.

Bombay Immigrant

He steps off the train
onto the crowded platform:
coolies in red shirts
squatting on dusty flagstones
smoking beedies*;
families scattered
among bedrolls and battered tin trunks
tied up with frayed nylon rope;
hawkers baying and yelling,
selling everything from toothbrushes
to melting ice cream.

Gaggle of sights.
Village memories
shunted into the back of his mind:
the smoky smell of burning cow dung,
the sound of a bucket falling into the well,
the wheat swishing in the field.

He walks out of the station
past the two stone lions
guarding the gate of Victoria Terminus.
He sees his reflection in a shopwindow
and even to himself,
it is new.

---

*An Indian cigarette that has no filter—just tobacco wrapped in a leaf. Cheaper than Western-style cigarettes, beedies are smoked mostly by the average Indian.

Learning Persian

A hibernating language
lying in the dark corners of my mind,
awakens slowly after a ten-year sleep.

Naked,
bones creaking,
it crawls forward,
searching for lost pieces of clothing
in forgotten nooks and crannies.

Ragged and unkempt,
it finally tries to rise.
It ventures out
on a wave of words.

The world lies before it
waiting to be sung.

Origin

I did not come on a midnight train
and not on a barge.
I cannot make it sound like the chains
that Africa cut loose to be free
on ships that no storm could devour.
I had not stolen a kiss from the snake,
and I did not fall out of my mother's womb.
If I had dreamt, it was not the golden dream
of any rush to fame or fortune.
I could not have rushed;
I was stalled on the rack of time
between two seas
that howled endlessly.

ALI ZARRIN

A Word with Majesty

After we whipped the sea in a foreign land,
our children wept every night for a piece of bread.
What glories did you bring, Xerxes,
beyond a silk coffin?
What glories other than a golden tomb?

Three thousand years of bloodbath!
Three thousand years of wild poppies
grown in the desert,
three thousand years of the sound of a harp
coming from an unknown cave or a grave!
Who taught us to write poetry with our blood?

Hafez must have understood Khayyam well.
His wine is pouring from the same jug
that was once filled with blood shed by the Tartars,
and takes its daily fill from Nishapur.
When Mazdak spoke of equality
he must have known we have the same blood color.

After we lit the first fire to burn forever,
after we endured the sun, and took water for mirror,
our hearts have gone ablaze.

Made You Mine, America

America
in the poems of Walt Whitman
Langston Hughes
Allen Ginsberg
the songs of Woody Guthrie
and Joan Baez
I made you mine

rushing to you
at night and daybreak
by air and water—
on the land
getting a social security number
in the year nineteen hundred seventy
working the grave-
yard shift for ITT
a teenager four levels below the ground
a cashier in a three-by-eight booth
under the Denver Hilton Hotel
sheltering derelicts
who slept on beds
of cardboard and newspaper
pillows of shoes
my young body luring
late-night prostitutes and transvestites
hip to my accent
the midnight thief

pouring Mace in my eyes
escaping
up the long ramp

passing through barbed wires
and waiting for hours in the INS lobbies
facing grouchy secretaries
overwhelmed by the languages
they can't speak and accents
they can't enjoy
becoming naturalized
in the year of bicentennial celebration

the migration of my parents
to your welfare state
of millions living
in tenement housing
reeking with the smell of urine
and cheap liquor

traveling
the US of A
as large as Whitman's green mind
white beard and red heart
from the Deadman's Pass rest area
on the old Oregon Trail
to the Scenic Overlook at the Mason-Dixon line, Maryland
from Mountain Home—Idaho
to Rockford—Illinois
as large as Mark Twain's laughter and irony
from the YMCA's casket-size single rooms
in Brooklyn

Chicago
San Francisco
to Denver's Republic Hotel
the home of broken old men
and women subsisting on
three hundred sixty-four dollar
social security checks

waiting on
Denver oilmen in the Petroleum Club
nights of jazz at El Chapultepec
the Larimer of the past
where Arapahoes lived in their
teepees and now sleep
on the sidewalks
with battered lips
and broken heads

going door to door on Madison Avenue, Seattle
selling death insurance
for American National
servicing houses of bare minimum—
a TV and a couch
drunken men and women
lonely ailing old African
women making quilts
selling each
for fifty dollars

marrying a teacher
a third-generation auto worker

whose parents shared crops
in Caraway, Arkansas

fathering two tender boys
born in America
with their blue and brown eyes

substituting
for teachers
baby-sitting bored middle school children
driving them
home in a school bus
teaching your youth
to write English
and speak Persian

loving
your children
daughters
sons
mothers
fathers
grandmothers
grandfathers
hating your aggression
you aligned yourself with the worst
of my kind
exiled my George Washington—
Dr. Mohammad Mosaddeq—
helped Saddam bomb my birthplace
destroy the school of my childhood

his soldiers swarming the hills of Charzebar
where as a child I hunted
with my grandfather
sold arms to warmongers
who waged battles on grounds
on which my great-grandfather made
fifteen pilgrimages on foot
to Karbala

now I lay claim
to your Bill of Rights
and Declaration of Independence.

I came to you
not a prince
who had lost his future throne
not a thief finding
a cover in the multitudes
of your metropoles
hiding behind your volumes of law
not a merchant dreaming of exploiting
your open markets
not a smuggler
seeking riches overnight
but a greenhorn seventeen-year-old
with four hundred dollars
after Dad sold his prized Bretta rifle
and Mom some of her wedding jewelry
with a suitcase of clothes
and books—
Hafez
Rumi

Shakespeare
Nima
Forugh
and a small Qu'ran—
my grandmother's gift
not to conquer
Wall Street
Broadway
or Hollywood
I came to you to study
to learn
and I learned
you can't deny me parenthood
I lost my grandparents
while roaming your streets
traveling across your vastness
you can't turn me down
I gave you my youth
walking and driving Colfax nights long
I came with hate
but now
I love you
America.

Galloping: the original reds

I.   Blossom
     Blossom

     Nothing

     Turn

     Day

     — —

     girl lives in a shoe

     you should've brought your camera,
          fool

     smooth dune butts
     cigarette, an ocean ode
     the caretaker's daughter was well

     red and green silver moss dollars: canopy
                     panoply

     (India in an earlier year)

     — —

shapes
inside her rib cage: hot
wilted finger-flowers

then she is gone,   closer, closed

II.   girl lives in a shoe, or car
fakes an old love song
like a new leaf

the faces of asking,
a shiny conduct up

— —

Day
Day

Blossom

Nothing

Turn

III. I was the girl
I was the girl
in your eyes
your poor words
I saw your back

the girl in the two-part
dress at the morning intersection

Punching the punching bag,
you tell your brother. Let
them talk, the doctors—
she has breath
and we will watch her

then it's lovely
she goes from being an old neighbor   to being a new one

Elephants

me and 11,000 pounds
swaying
Botswana eyes

transmit, transmit

dome of light
zoo brick hut
finding the space between car and elephant,
        this, and child looks
and she finding what:
            child eyes

I remembered a poem
about tigers and Niagara
Falls, a honeymoon

parched skin
speckled trunk
forty years old

swaying
swaying, transmit
Botswana eyes

Baby by her side.
Legs straight out
when he's asleep,
rolls one red eye funny

(my husband in bed
beside me
his back turned to me)
the red and pink of this phrase
the light from the bathroom,
not because this is about
light,
makes it possible
for me to carry these things
in my head

I get out of my car at the zoo: elephant
                                polar bear
                                lover

finding your finger
the crease in your back
your back which knows nothing of porridge or purple

I sit poised on the bench
until I can't anymore,
and steam lives everywhere.

And then there's you.
The other side of you.
When I come to you,
your hands are good.
Your back sways.
There is a want like air.

This keeps me awake at nights:
the elephant's nails.

Hay, crusted.
Comic trunk. Order.

Your body in the light.
That you slept so easily,
were used to changing
seasons, your arm outheld.
The taste of tangerine
in my mouth at 4 A.M.

God in a funny pit
in my stomach:
Whom all this
is supposed to be about.

A circle of elephant,
two elephants, sweet
trunk, baby
a dark smudge,
gentle tusks,
mother swaying

speckled trunk
hollow forehead
ears like pastry

Hay. God in the other room,
in the corner of the swimming pool

my earnest

that we're ending we're ending.

No. 2

In Iran where there were mosaics of blue and white birds perched on bars all over our kitchen floor, and in the corner of the bakery filled with marzipan animals and sunlight, the dentist's office right above, *Maman's* open purse was a good sign, and she stood looking as if she were a smoker, which she wasn't, only waiting for us to choose, and we chose, feeling the matted form of a pig, a cow, or dog on our tongues, walking out onto the sidewalk in Tehran: happiness is an ice-cream cone, the song went: and we watched things rush past in the gutter, water running fast and high.

The car then moving through green and glen, my brother in the back seat, his hair in his face. A short name, Kia. It's just me and him and the company chauffeur, and we drive until we see the trees on the crooked road leading to school. Two children feeding on cheese puffs, orange fuzzes of nothing we daily discover in the glove compartment. Sweet tarts are the best, and every day Mr. Pishgah looks for them at the *baghali*. He is a hero in a hurry and can read great big maps and the minds of at least three cars ahead, shouting right or left before they turn. He calls us *modar*—mother—when we start to cross the street.

It's my brother who reminds me years later, says he thinks it was once just him and Mr. Pishgah, sitting and talking with the windows rolled down. I see a smudge of a boy in shorts and saddle shoes, a few bad words in his vocabulary, gliding in the back seat of that car, in the haze and dust and breeze, with just that man for company. What vicious denials of origin and first loves, a nanny and chauffeur from twenty years before. Unbearable how much I loved you and didn't say it. How I thought the world ended in you.

untitled

In my one dream of you, I've driven miles
with no radio on, fingers to lips, unquiet,
past rails and rails, then summer, juniper,
to find you at work in a small blue hospital.
I say: Come sit next to me on the curb outside
where we are both nobodies
and tell me that I am dead to you
or that you are dead to me,
but tell me:
for someone has asked me to marry
and I am one leg gone this time, I swear it.

Only then, there is a field of slivered almonds,
teeming white, and we stand: two soft figures
in blue-green: knights. You
hand me a note, the faintest lines.

You have hoarded all these months
and I am so angry, I want to be you. But
you do not save me, and neither do these words.
And then I remember that I'm not looking
to be saved, anyway.   (The happening: almost: trees)

The Untimely Traveler

untimely traveler
I am the last child;
in search of the origins of my belatedness,
forever wandering the alleys of desire
and streets of wonder . . .

My father
might have been the Spaniard
who died fighting the revolutionary wars
and my mother
the Goddess of the hunt and the moon
who carried torches in her hand
followed by untamed animals.

I once knew a young man
who drowned himself in the moon
as his heart discovered
   its fullness
    at the heights
      of blue seashores;
and I know of a woman
who remained a virgin till the age of 64
    (and she died
      of a massive heart attack).

Often I come home
and discover silence

greeting me at the door.
Why should I worry
if the answering machine forgets to blink
or if the postman arrives
     empty-handed?
Why should I care
if my questions scratch
   the borderlines of categories
or if definitions do not suffice?
Why should I change
if you call me too sensitive
because I cry at the funeral of pigeons
who were crushed
   by the ruthless tires of automobiles?

Often I wake up
and instead of sunrise
three sunflowers rise
behind the horizon of a wooden frame,
the mirror yawns at my face
as the toothbrush gets prepared
for another ritual
   of rubbing against hardness.

Often I hide
behind the purple shelter of the curtains
to watch the pensive passerby
who follows the footprints of the street-cat
that after a long snowy night
has pioneered the discovery of dawn.

I am the last witness
forever musing on the cradle of myth
    and hands of memory
in search of the martyr
who was buried within the chest of time.

I saw Moses last night
melancholic
    at the street corner café,
shedding tears for his abandoned infancy
over streams of the Nile;
and I asked him
what the world would've been like
had Abraham decided
at the sacrificial moment
    between Isaac and Ishmael.

I am the last note
waiting to be played
pleading with you not to question
why at the height of musical moments
pleasure diffuses into mist
or teardrops fall
    into the open curve
        of joyous smiles . . .

Often I sit down
at the crossroads of a day;
the afternoon departs me
while poetry arrives.
Why should I regret
if at those very moments

my shoulders should feel the poverty
    of another's
        loving kiss?

The world thus recedes
at the impromptu poetic creation,
love engulfs everything
and matters cease to exist
    as they used to be . . .

I am the last child;
in search of the origins of my belatedness
forever searching
    all corners of desire
        and the endless roads
            of wonder . . .

Season of Revival

I never heard the humming of the new season
which had calmly arrived
at the gate of my old
    garden of wishes.

That day
you took me on an afternoon stroll
and showed me orchids and azaleas
where only jasmines used to grow;
then you believed in my dreams
and I harvested crops of grapes and plums
from the heart of old cactuses
    and dead trees.
"Has this frog been here forever?"
    you mumbled in wonderment
and I pointed toward the orange tree,
"Where did that child go
    who used to play over there?"

The blue in your dreams
thus turned into green
and the weight in my wings
bowed toward my feet
which had begun befriending
the moisture in the soil
    and the roughness of stones.

Up in the mountains
rests a proud opera house
where peacocks attend and squirrels clap.
In between redwoods
the round face of the moon reigns.
"Does it envy the earthly rust of the jungle
Or is it heavenly like youth
waning when it is fullest?"

Down in the garden
night lazily falls
onto the lap of the Sunday afternoon
yawning in boredom of a day
    of champagne and barbecue.
The fire is barely alive
and I smell
  the closing of an old era.

The evening breeze,
    the caress,
the freckled face of a boy
  with far-fetched fantasies of puberty.
Mother blows the last *poke* of her cigarette
into the face of curious stars;
Father covets the grace of sky
gently grabbing stripes of smoke
   entangled into the vertical time.

"Who's made the moon so round,
        Mommy?"
Then the streaking sound of the garage door

the flight of a blue jay;
the sudden reality of an oak tree
        standing alone,
and the inevitable liberty
    of a drop
        of dew.

"To what does the evening star hang on?"
The man grins,
extinguishing his pipe,
and the woman gets up
heading off toward the mountains,
        standing proud
            and away.

By the mountainside lives an old man
who milks cows in the morning,
plays his pipe in the afternoon
and lets the crickets sing him to sleep.
Everyday
he builds a new window
with blinds of memory
and thin curtains
colored with
    untainted shades of love.
Travelers bring him fruit jam and chestnuts
and he tells them of his revolutionary past
with small wishes
    the size of a decent home
and simple hopes
as warm as the fresh bread
you take each morning with your tea.

Down the stream
grow tiny purple flowers;
they call them "Persian nights"
and I look for a trace of mockingbird nearby.
You pick a bunch
in memory of the young woman
who left one night
in search of the morning star;
and I turn around
to break the bubble glass
where I had kept for so many years
a bundle of colored wishes
and a few dry butterflies . . .

SOLMAZ SHARIF

My Father's Shoes

They were my father's shoes.
My mother looked at them and saw a donation to Goodwill.
My father looked at them and saw his life.
They were there with him on his last step in his home country.
They were there with him when he first saw me.
They kissed the dirt of the "land of opportunity."

My mother looks at them and sees dust collectors.
My fathers sees his first day at work.
He sees his graduation.
He sees the hard work it took to get those shoes.

My mother looks at them and sees things that take up extra space.
I don't look at the shoes.
My father's face says it all.

ZJALEH HAJIBASHI

Morning Exercise

Three trees mark the start
it's 5 A.M.
not that cold, but dark
my jogging suit
a long black coat and scarf.

My uncle and I run
from street corner
to
street corner—
a quarter mile stretch—
scuffled steps and
steady even breaths
the only noise.
We don't speak,
do not disturb the
morning,
still asleep.
But at every turn, Persian words
punctuate the trees
I'm learning to read.

In the spring the
lines were scarcely there,
fractured shapes
buried and meaningless
beneath the overhanging mass

of streetlamp
mottled green.

Now the lights expose
thick letters:
MRG is scrawled between the trunks
below naked knotted limbs
that strain to hold
absolutely
nothing
up.

MRG is death
its vowel understood
the word does not stay flat—
spray-painted, chanted, adulated
the letters broad and animated
Marg waves at every parade
riding on sticks
up and down
poking
gaping
huge
holes in the air
the people are trying to breathe.
I've never seen death like this
so quick
so popular
so proudly posed
for every photograph.

Nearing the turn,
My arms drop
closed fists
open hands
those letters
three
behind
the pallid trees lined up
against the wall
I run
past.

Hybrid

By the time I figured out
what made an Iranian girl
good
it was too late.
I had already been corrupted by America,
her loose hips and ungracious manner
had watered me down further.
I couldn't even be called "Iranian-American"
I lacked the sensibility, the language,
the distaste for body hair
and the desire for a small nose.
It was too late . . . I'd already
become something else
and couldn't read the codes
one needs
to function
as an Iranian.
It was bad enough that I had four brothers
and a mother who wasn't glamorous,
I had learned to curse and cared more
about grades than boys.
Occasionally, when I didn't do what he wanted
my father reminded me
that I was *too* American . . .
a phrase that cut like a dagger
against the skin,
separated me out

and drove a wedge
between us.
I could never quite figure out how much
was too American.
Did he mean, don't disrespect your parents,
tell them everything,
don't sleep with a boy
before marriage,
don't give yourself too easily?
Did he mean that my American part
should not disobey *his* law?
It was too late.
Like all immigrant parents, he wants me to succeed,
to get an education, to be smart and beautiful
but not to forget
that I had to find a man.
"Women are like fruit trees," he said, "they have to bear children
    or they'll wither."
When he put it like that,
all I wanted was to be
one of those hybrid
ornamental plums
whose blossoms are sweet and glorious
but fall to the ground
without ever bearing fruit.

SANAZ NIKAEIN

Exile

Thrilled to go on a vacation
in the middle of the school year
to a village hours away.

Too young to understand
the entire city of Tehran
warned of Iraqi missiles and bombs
looked for shelter elsewhere.

⤷ SAÏDEH PAKRAVAN ⤸

Mother, Mother

When you found me
folded in a poppy at the top of the hill
my lids so smooth and my nails so pale
did you know then that we would come this far
wander these many years and more

that we would rehearse this long day's journey
as though a life would be given us once more

did you know then that we never grow wise
but do indeed grow bored
that the thumb we suck one day no longer comforts
that the music in clubs one night is too loud
that illness happens mother, mother,
that few friends remain
and what we believe in
we have to create

as we spread before our feet a road to walk on
smoothing out potholes
yet still surprised
to find ourselves tripping
tripping.

Uzumborun

See how tall Damavand stands, its head
held high above the clouds. It is silver haired
even in this green season. The sun
reflects off the tangled locks that fall
on the mountain's broad, colorless shoulders.

Damavand had been like this long before
you and I first looked up at its heights.

Snow clings to the summit's every rise and fold
like an old man's wrinkled face, lined
by the contours of age: strong, northern
features, angular nose and sunken eyes
that seem to squint under the sun and swell
with tears; tears that slowly drip and at times,
with a flashing wink, catch a fleeting ray.

Soon, quiet streams will roll down the snowy face
and rocky bosom through deliberate lines
carved long ago. They follow their own
ancient routes to a calm, expectant pool,
join and gather force before tumbling toward
the valley below that lies cradled in shadows.

And at the mountain's foot, the Caspian—
this giant lake, this gentle sea—awaits
the rushing waters so that it may feed

its depths. There, hidden from our eyes
suckles the sturgeon, queen Uzumborun,
blessed with the gift of laying golden eggs.

Unlike you and me who watch from afar,
her fate lies in the strong and weathered hands
of the old fisherman who slowly drags
his net, taut with the Caspian's riches,
onto the unyielding sand. And with it
the sturgeon is drawn to the edge of her world.

She breaks the surface to a place rounded
at the edges, and with a silent gasp
pumps her gills with inaccessible air.
Suddenly aware of her own weight, she
strains to return to the cool depths of home
and lay her golden eggs, which now
belong neither to herself
nor to the fisherman.

⊱ REZA ASHRAH ⊰

and

⊱ MICHAEL C. WALKER ⊰

blindness of our depth

were you there in the morning?
when opened like a circle was
the heart of purple, was the princely sun?
did you pause to tremble
as holiness was unexpected like
my present fear is provided now to me?
like scorn is plenty for the gliding serpent,
was that land alone enough to suffice?

ambergris in my youth is your saliva,
from what I make the imperfect wonder.
balm in this torn youth is your own fear,
from what I make peace to my nerves compared.
fatwa is represented now by your skin,
when no other regent could for me be found.
as a pomegranate is burst on burlap and stains,
our young silk is burdened by the unspeakable.

an ewer engraved with the letters of your name,
would not be less of an emblem of iniquity than
a silver trumpet in the evening would be of mirth;
so I tend to take my symbols gingerly into the night.

I can't stand it but I do endure this,
I can't reason it alive but won't allow it to die,
I can't piece any justice to its implacable frame.

I am calling you as voices also call me:
bacheh baz, no matter, for it is the same.
upon my bed forlorn and staring into the dark,
I shiver for the periodical lacking,
I shiver for the fearsome attendance
of reality into the blindness of our depth.

were you ever more than tremulous in that place?
were you allowed by your acrid mind to think aloud
without remembering your choking sky,
your garlands of words and unclean eyes,
your asking for the permission never alive?

❅ Short Stories ❅

ZJALEH HAJIBASHI

Heaven's Fruit

Why didn't it ring? Late afternoon was the very worst time of day. She tugged another loose string from the red flower pattern on the faded rug beneath her round stockinged foot. Street noises didn't reach her anymore, but she could still hear the front door open and close, the signal to gather her chador and drape it over her swollen, purple corpuscled knees. Her son would be home soon. He would poke his head through her slightly cracked door and say "*Salaam*," then she'd hear his sandals slapping up the stairs and she'd be alone again. She pulled the telephone closer. The numbers on the beige dial were almost completely worn away. She picked up her telephone book filled with large numbers, in a child's hand or her own, awkward marks scrawled in pencil. She flipped through the book that was no longer bound together, order preserved only by the big rubber band she wrapped around it when it was closed. The names were arranged according to her own design and did not match the index tabs on the edges of each page. Perhaps she would call her sister-in-law, who was still trying to get over her oldest daughter's death from a terrible . . . cold. No one ever named what had taken Nahid's chest and then her life away. That would be like saying a woman in the family had lost face. So many things just should never be said. She'd lost her own eldest daughter the same way. Her hand rested softly on the receiver. "God always picks the most lovely flowers first." There were a limited number of things she could say and she'd said them already, over and over again. Mostly she would listen, then the two of them would cry and console one another. Their conversations had been pretty much the same for months now. She drew her hand into her lap. Perhaps it would be better to call tomorrow, it was time for tea now anyway.

Without getting up, she scooted over to the small gas stove at the front of the room by the glass doors, took a big wooden match out of the box she kept tucked under the heater, and lit the flame of her one burner stove. She poured water from a plastic pitcher into the kettle already sitting in its place. Her youngest granddaughter filled the pitcher for her every morning. Who would have thought she could love a girl so much? Her own daughters had waited on her all her life, but she had never hidden the fact that she loved her sons, two of them half a world away, a great deal more. No doubt it was bitterness from a lifetime of being loved less that kept her next to oldest daughter from treating her with greater kindness. From time to time, Zahra still brought dishes that she especially liked, but it had been Zahra who had maneuvered Reza and his family into her house so that his young wife could take over most of the work involved in caring for her now that she was floor-bound. Every morning about eight, Zahra would call and ask how she was and they'd talk for a half-hour or more on the phone even though her house was just down the street, a short walk away. Her granddaughter was more precious to her than her own daughters for sure. Almost five now, Behdokht was her grand-mother's right hand and both feet. When her son had called with news of Behdokht's birth, she had blessed her granddaughter's arrival grudgingly with her "I'm disappointed it's a girl" tone of voice. But this little girl was something else altogether. Whenever her son and his wife wanted to go out, they'd leave their tiny baby in her lap. The two developed an amazing rapport, shared a secret language of ges-tures and expressions. Tiny Behdokht listened to her more patiently than anyone but God.

After she put the tea on to steep, she would get ready for afternoon prayers. Unless she was too sick to move she never missed them. "Y'Ali," she would say, and with tremendous effort, she would roll over on her knees and start making her way on all fours to the faucet her son who lived in the States had installed by her room. She said a prayer for him every single time she used it. But even though she was glad not to have to depend on someone for help all the time, she missed having someone come down to pour warm water over her hands. She ran them both under the faucet then splashed water on her face and wiped it off, running her forefinger and thumb from her forehead to her chin. The rest of her ablutions varied, sometimes they were less than ideal, it depended on how she was feeling. Was that the phone ringing? It never failed. Someone always called when she was washing or praying. She swallowed her disappointment. Whoever it was would call back, she would just have to wait. She dried off with a small hand towel then crawled back to her room, careful to keep her chador under her hands until she reached the threshold. She kept her prayer stone and beads wrapped in a washrag she brought back from America ten years ago. The tag was still attached, "Sears Best." She set the small bundle on an old three-legged stool that was just the right height for her to rest her head on when she bent at the waist. Then she tied her dark blue chador, covered with tiny white flowers, close around her face and knotted it beneath her chin. The words of her prayers never changed but every time she repeated them she said something different. After all the ritual prostrations, she stared straight ahead through the glass doors, passing the clay beads from hand to hand, counting out her thanks to God. She wrapped the beads in a ring around the stone, wiped away the tear lines on her face and folded up her light blue washrag.

It had been five years since she'd been outside. She cracked the door open as far as the bars would allow; a gentle breeze blew softly against her face. The bars and an ugly building blocked her view of the sky. Both had gone up just after the revolution when there was no one to police the zoning or the streets. She could walk then and had lived alone in her three-story house. If it weren't for the neighbor who'd yelled out, she was sure the man who had crawled over the wall into her courtyard would have slit her throat from ear to ear. Still, she wished the bars weren't there now.

She opened the red checkered plastic table cloth. This morning's bread was folded in a neat pile square in the middle. She picked up her favorite tea cup from a tray and spooned in half an inch of sugar, stirring briskly as she poured herself some tea. A piece of bread would take the edge off until dinnertime. Sometimes she would pull some sequestered sweet from the cubbyholes behind her, but usually, except for bread, she ate only when her family fed her. These past few years she's been steadily losing weight. From the time she was a little girl she had been big. She loved good food, and being from a well-to-do family, she had always been surrounded by delicious things to eat. What she wouldn't give for a decent meal dripping with lard instead of hardened vegetable oil. No matter how many spoonfuls went in, the food never tasted fat. Cooks had done all the work, but after she was married at the age of twelve she was responsible for keeping everything running smoothly. To earn the servants' respect, she had been exceedingly harsh.

She gathered the loose scraps of bread into a pile and tossed them onto the porch for the sparrows. Had those days been just a dream?

The clouds were shading the sky smooth and gray. Only a few minutes remained until the evening call for prayer. She prayed afternoon and evening prayers almost back-to-back. Two for one. There was a limit to the number of trips she could make to the faucet. A car eased into the driveway. Reza was home. He stepped out of the car, opened the back, and picked up two bags. She watched him walk toward the door—his hair, like hers, was as white as snow.

She hears the door open and the sound of her son's humming. He breaks off the tune but with the same lilt calls out loud, "Salaam, Furugh jun!" She sees the back of his jacket as he comes around the corner and sets the sacks heavily on the table. "Have I got something for

you today!" He turns around to face her carrying three huge red pomegranates in both hands. He steps inside her room and places them on
the table cloth; his eyes dance. "I'll be back in awhile." Picking up the
sacks, Reza heads up the stairs. She watches him go, looks long and
hard at the heavy, perfectly ripe fruit, then ties her chador under her
chin again for sunset prayers. As darkness falls, her spirits lift. Everyone is home. She hears their footsteps above her and her room feels
cozy, not like a cage, even in the dark. Her son, pomegranate juicer
and paper in hand, comes in and turns on the light. For him, her room
is a quiet refuge, the best place to read the evening news. But first
things first. He spreads an old newspaper out on the floor and cuts
each fruit in half, the juice from each slice soaks into the paper, deep
burgundy-red. Reza sets a clear glass beneath the spout, puts the
pomegranate on the metal point and presses; the tiny seeds crunch
and juice runs out. When the small glass is full, he passes it to his
mother, the sleeve of his old baby blue sweater hangs loose around
his hand. He fills another glass for himself, crumples up the old paper
and spreads out the new one. He sits cross-legged, in loose pajama
pants, not quite directly across from his mother. She sips at the
sweetness as she watches her son pore over each page. She knows exactly how many times to interrupt without being rude. He chooses a
few articles to read out loud but is careful not to bore her. She looks
at the photos. Even upside down, pictures of Rafsanjani make her
chuckle, "Who ever thought a *mullah* would be king?" Her son was
in a good mood; soon, he would yell upstairs to his wife to bring dinner. Even with the children's help, it was a big production to get
everything downstairs. She knew Reza was caught in the middle between his concern for her and for his wife's feelings. At lunchtime,
his wife or daughter would take a plate downstairs piled high with
rice and some succulent sauce. Like her own daughter, her daughter-
in-law went to extra trouble to make the food she liked best; but
truth was, she had come to prefer fried eggs and potatoes to those

painstakingly prepared lunches she almost always ate alone. Behdokht set her place, pushed aside the telephone, and sat down close
beside her, close enough that they touched. She looked down at her
granddaughter's small head; her hair was so shiny and black. The little girl turned and looked up into her grandmother's eyes. "Do you
want something *Maman Buzurg?*" She patted Behdokht gently on the
head. "No, nothing Nana, just eat your food." Sweet like honey this
one was, not like other girls.

After supper was cleared away, she ventured into the hallway again
to wash her hands and rinse her mouth. Back in her room, on hands
and knees she unrolled her thin mattress and her sheet and spread.
Whoever thought she would have to make up her own bed? She hears
someone outside her room. Like a blind woman, she recognizes her
grandchildren by the sound of their steps. "Husayn *jun*, bring me a little water dear." He walks to the refrigerator, pours her a tall glass and
takes it to her room, "Here *Maman Buzurg*, I brought it for you." He
sets it down beside her bed and turns out the light. Without raising
her head from the pillow, she thanks him and says, "*Shab beh khayr,*"
sleep well.

She lay awake awhile thinking of favorite places she'd been, Taj-
rish, Mashhad, Jerusalem, Mecca, even Las Vegas. She dreamed
about those people she missed, her children mostly, or simple pleasures like steam-filled lazy half-days at the baths.

The morning sun hit her full in the face. She'd long since stopped
trying to rise before dawn—her body ached too much. She did her
best to greet the day with a grateful heart, but it was getting more
and more difficult. When would her soul be clean enough for God to
take? Each day she felt passed over. Surely by now the thorns had
dried up and fallen off.

Martyrdom Street

Buildings. Everywhere you look, there are buildings. On Inqilab Avenue two solitary walls stand upright on the left side of the road. It's anybody's guess what this pile of rubble will turn out to be. Maybe the government has commissioned a mosque, a business center, or a mall. Or better yet, a monument honoring the dead. The drilling sounds subside as I move beyond the construction zone. Ali Agha, the baker, spits out orange seeds on the cracked cement as he counts some change in his hand. Come to think of it, even his store is a new addition to the street.

"What time is it?" Ali Agha asks a worker as he observes the pedestrians on the opposite corner. The worker tells him the time from inside the bread shop. "It's slow again today," he says, mostly to himself. When he recognizes a customer, Ali Agha motions to his cronies to bring out the sheets of warm *lavash*. "Hurry up! Hurry up!" he yells, now sitting erect on the edge of his chair. As the customer approaches, Ali Agha holds out the bread and says, "Fresh out of the oven. Don't you want to take some home to your wife?" The pedestrian lowers his head, quickly walking away, and Ali Agha curses at a young employee before eating the bread himself. "How am I supposed to run a business?" he complains. "What's their excuse now? The war has long been over."

As I walk past the bread shop, Ali Agha notices me, and the scene repeats itself. "I was waiting for you," he says, rising from his chair. "Some bread, *Haji Khanum*?" I don't fault Ali Agha for his sycophantic manners. He smiles. He calls me "*Haji Khanum*." He politely holds out the bread. The economy is hard on everybody these days.

"Six sheets of *lavash*," I say.

When I hand him the change, Ali Agha takes my good hand and kisses it. "God bless you!" he exclaims, following up the blessing with a token prayer, but I quickly pull my hand away. Ali Agha apologizes, and I walk away quickly. So quickly that I don't realize I've walked past the post office. I wipe my good hand against my Islamic attire, rubbing it hard into the cloth until I see a spot of blood. I know then that I've atoned for the sin. It's un-Islamic to touch a man's hand. These are the fine points we learned in school; fine points about nails and skin and hair and water and dirt and cotton and wood. Where religion is concerned, there's always something new to learn.

I pass Ali Agha's bread shop every Tuesday en route to the downtown post office. Since the explosion, I've had a lot of free time on my hands, so I create mindless chores for myself. I feed the pigeons. I water the gardens. Or I visit the post office. Nowadays, the post office certifies all our letters and packages. Letters with pictures in them or letters with little substance. Perfunctory letters about the weather or the new ice-cream store down the block. My daughter, Nasrin, lives in America, but she probably can't read Persian anymore, so why waste time crafting a masterpiece? Still, I prefer descriptive missives myself. Long letters about winter nights in cold gardens, but Nasrin rarely writes back. When she makes the effort, it hardly seems worth the trouble. Her last one arrived three months ago. I've memorized its notable passages: "Hamid looks like Husni Mubarak. I think it's the nose." Hamid is her fiancé. Then she adds, "Are you still praying, Maman?" I'll keep her letter in my purse until the next one arrives.

Today, I take the long route to the post office: through the bazaar and past Muhsin's engineering building. I haven't been to this part of town since the last months of the war . . . has it already been a year?

Anyhow. That day, too, I stopped by the bazaar. I wanted a merchant there to price some of our family antiques. They were for Nasrin, and I thought she might want them someday for her home. I don't know what I was thinking, since leaving Iran wasn't an imminent possibility back then, with the war dragging on, no end in sight. But in a state of war, denying reality comes more easily than embracing the truth. So I asked the merchant if he'd be willing to smuggle out the antiques for a modest bribe. He just rolled his eyes and sighed.

Disappointed, I left the bazaar for the post office. A long line curved around the outside of the building, but, compared to the gasoline lines, this one moved swiftly. As I walked in, the mosque projected the noontime prayer call, the *azan*, which echoed in the neighborhood, and a young woman behind me silently mouthed her prayers. Outside, military planes flew low, circling the neighborhood; only the *azan* muffled their distant drone. When the prayer call finally ended, the young woman started speaking softly to me. "They recruited my youngest son for the war," she said. "He's twelve. Do you have a son?"

I shook my head.

Then she whispered, "I don't believe in martyrdom."

Before I could respond, an altercation broke out between two customers standing ahead of us in line. "It's my turn," a bearded middle-aged man declared as he elbowed a *chadori* woman half his size to claim a spot in front of the post-office clerk.

"What do you mean?" the woman challenged. "I've been waiting for twenty minutes." As she was speaking, the woman adjusted her black veil to hide loose strands of hair. Then, she turned to the person behind her to say, "Didn't you see him just walk in the door?" But no one rushed to support her. Maybe it was the desperation in her voice, the hypocrisy of her wearing a chador, or the assumption of the weakness of her gender that made her appear guilty. Even though the woman was telling the truth, she appeared less sincere than the man.

The post-office clerk intervened to resolve the situation. "Khanum," he said to the chador-clad woman, "please cooperate. Let this man finish his business. You'll be next." Before the woman could voice another complaint, there was a loud thud. It was a noise I'd never heard before—as if twenty trucks had crashed into one another. From a distance the red-alert signals, which sounded like truncated ambulance sirens, began to toll. The Iraqis had struck something, but nobody seemed to know what.

Helicopters had joined the military planes to survey the streets. Inside, no one dared speak, except for the post-office clerks, who shouted orders to file people out of the building. "Over here," a young man yelled, and we formed a line behind him. Another loud crash shook the main lobby, and the concrete beneath our feet began to tremble. The young woman standing behind me again prayed silently as she watched a rat scuttle across the floor. Before the rat reached the western end of the lobby, the tiles trembled, and we flew out of the building.

That's all I remember about that Tuesday afternoon. I'm not even sure if the ground was really shaking after the third blast, or whether my knees were betraying me. I'm not sure. Everything happened quickly, maybe within five minutes.

An old man sits in a wheelchair outside the post-office entrance—a spot he's claimed since the war. I place the warm sheets of *lavash* in his lap and step into the building. He mumbles some incoherent words, and I turn around to acknowledge his disjointed utterances, but I know his memory will only register the incident for a few short minutes. As I wait in line, two teenage boys push ahead of me, but I don't see any point in fighting such aggression. Moralizing won't persuade them to change their habits.

When the post-office clerk finally registers my letter, I step outside and walk a short distance. The man in the wheelchair has managed to roll himself a block farther, and when I approach him, he doesn't recognize me. He reaches out for change, and I place a fifty-toman bill in his lap. At the first green light I catch a bus, and from the window I observe other reconstruction projects throughout the city.

The government rebuilt the post office six months ago. A businessman who'd lost a son in the war donated large sums of money to renovate the building. For days, construction workers toiled to efface all remnants of the explosion, burying broken bones and torn clothing under the ground. Still, despite its bright clean walls, fragrant household plants, and new faces, this building doesn't differ much from the old one.

Only scattered ruins in the southern corners of the city linger as icons of the war. A chipped wall, a shattered window, a cripple. Where rocks and gravel once covered the streets, new monuments stand in their places. Outside the main drive leading to the post office, schoolchildren gather regularly to water fresh flowers. On that street, Martyrdom Street, where tulips bloom perennially, only the murmurs of the dead keep their memories alive.

I decide to take a detour and step off the bus to visit the *Imam's* tomb. Despite the summer drought, a gardener lavishly waters a fresh flower patch next to the sanctuary, but no one seems to mind. In the courtyard a mother rocks her newborn son and hums a gentle lullaby. The baby stares into the distance, through the massive columns and their plaster moldings. When the humming stops and the preacher's voice rises, the infant shifts in his mother's arms and wails.

"Maybe he's hungry," someone remarks.

"Or tired," another surmises.

"Here, *Khanum*, have some bread and cheese."

I go inside the shrine and walk toward the *Imam's* tomb. The smell of rosewater permeates the hand-woven rugs on the floor. Next to me, a woman wails and kisses the iron grids that protect the tomb, asking for miracles. I try hard to imitate her piety but can't. Her crying makes me nervous, and I decide to leave. Outside, a security guard approaches and removes his shoes by the entrance to the tomb. Today, he's only an ornament here. He doesn't see the young girl and teenage boy flirt while sharing a bowl of pistachios. The girl's veil slowly slides down her head, exposing thick black curls, but nobody chastizes her. The price of bread went up another ten tomans; the price of gasoline another five.

I catch the next bus and go home. There's nothing more to see here. The twenty-second of *Bahman* has become just another meaningless national holiday, like the commemorations of *Imams* or the birthdays of kings. My hand has started to ache, so I take some pills and wait for today to spill into tomorrow. Muhsin is gone and won't return for hours. I won't remember him coming home.

❦ ❦ ❦

The sky is still black, but morning lies just around the corner. Outside, the trees and crickets hide from view, conspiring to delay the arrival of dawn. I open the bedroom window and listen to their movements. I don't know how Muhsin lives with his other wife—where he sleeps, whether he leaves the window open or shut—but I don't speculate. This is my preferred hour of the day, when the streets are quiet and I can watch Muhsin dream. He doesn't feel me stroke his fingers.

From the bedside window, rays of light slowly penetrate the bedroom. I place my prayer rug in the middle of the room and begin the *namaz*. The obligatory prayers are brief, but I linger minutes longer to think. Last week, I found the opium stashed away in Muhsin's coat pocket but feigned ignorance. It's easier to keep up the pretense.

As I put away my prayer rug, Muhsin wakes up prematurely from his sleep. His forehead is covered in sweat and he throws the blanket off his body.

"It was hot," he says. "I felt like I was on fire."

"But the window is open," I say.

"I don't know. I was sweating uncontrollably."

"Where were you?" I ask.

"I'm not too sure. Near the *Takht-i Jamshid*. Under the rubble."

"It was only a dream," I assure him.

But he remains agitated and confused.

"Is the radio on?"

"No," I say. "It's early. Go back to sleep."

The samovar brews slowly in the kitchen. I set the breakfast plates and some *lavash* on the table. Muhsin joins me shortly with a cigarette in his hand. He appears more at ease, no doubt relieved to put the night behind him. Since my accident, his nightmares have become more frequent, but we don't always know what causes them.

Muhsin walks over to the counter to turn up the volume on the radio. When the announcer initiates a litany of doleful Arabic prayers, he reaches for an old newspaper on the kitchen table. "Nobody cares about the news anymore. All we hear these days are Arabic prayers. What's the matter with Persian? I bet they're afraid people might actually understand the nonsense they're promoting."

"They're just harmless prayers," I say. "Why make such a fuss?"

I place a cup of tea in front of him. Muhsin smirks at me but doesn't respond. Instead, he fiddles with the short-wave stations until he locates the BBC. Then he relaxes his forehead and continues eating his breakfast. "Much better," he comments, listening attentively to the news summaries, even though there's nothing noteworthy going on in the world. When the news hour is over, Muhsin goes into the bedroom to change. He yells to me from there and presses me to finish the cleaning quickly. I pretend not to hear him and sing to myself, louder and louder, until he's forced to repeat himself. Then he marches back into the kitchen and threateningly hovers over me.

"What?" I ask.

Muhsin pauses. He moves back slightly and starts drying the dishes.

"Nothing," he says. "I just don't us want to be late."

What is it about the air of guilt—the self-conscious twitches, the wandering eyes, and the cautious humor—that invariably gives the guilty away?

With Muhsin, it started with the smell of his cigarettes. Just before my accident, I noticed that his cigarettes no longer released the crisp aroma of fine tobacco. This was the smell of infirmity, the stench of tobacco grown on diseased lands. Maybe Iraqi shelling had damaged the yearly crop, transferring rare viruses from decaying human flesh onto idle land. Or maybe poor manufacturing had stained the tobacco leaves with unwelcome impurities. Pesticides. Fossil fuels. Chemical gas. Whenever Muhsin lit a cigarette, a grayish brown smoke stretched out sideways, and like a sick cat, he coughed endlessly and uncontrollably.

On that sunny afternoon when the post office was bombed, Muhsin had planned to spend the day working at his engineering firm. This line of work had irregular hours. Sometimes, during the week, Muhsin would be gone all morning; other times he wouldn't even leave the house. I watched him leave the house with his cigarettes and fake leather briefcase.

When the bombing threw me onto the concrete, I lay still, thinking of Muhsin. Random scenes passed before my eyes, and I could feel his presence. We were both downtown, maybe just a few streets away from each other. On a map of Tehran the distance between us measured less than the width of two fingers. I wondered whether Muhsin could hear me if I called out his name. Once or twice, I opened my mouth, but there was nothing. Tall flames spilled out of the sky, and I had difficulty focusing. I was slipping out of consciousness.

During my subsequent phase of alertness I smelled death. A young man lay beside me, breathing with prodigious effort, until he decided, quite abruptly, that life was no longer worth it. That was when I became aware of him—of his separated limb and gory perspiration. Dismembered from the rest of him, the man's hand had landed next to my feet. His was a beautiful hand with long artistic fingers and unmanicured nails, a hand capable of painting masterpieces or composing epics. He saw me admire his detached appendage and smiled vaguely. Just at that second, before he decided to surrender his body, his eyes caught mine. They seemed to tell me, "Take it, if that's what you want. It belongs to you now." I've often wondered about him and that hand.

A rescue worker draped a white sheet over his corpse and severed parts when the young man shut his eyes. I shifted slightly as the rescuer's shoes brushed against my side. Then the rescuer placed two fingers on my throat and yelled to his fellow workers, "This one's alive." Two helpers crossed the street and rushed to lift my body onto a wooden stretcher. "Does it hurt?" one of them asked, as he placed me inside the ambulance. It was his question that reminded me of the sensation I'd lost in my left hand.

A female attendant nurse rubbed an acrid liquid under my nose as the engine started. "Breathe," she said, gently caressing my face. When my inhalations grew regular, the woman raised my head to cover it with a veil. As she fastened the ends of the black fabric into a loose knot, she pledged, "Have faith, sister. We'll win the war," but her assistant just bandaged my hand and sneered. What did faith have to do with war?

Someone tried calling Muhsin at the office when we reached the hospital. Nothing major, they had claimed, which was true—just a deep wound in my left hand. As the doctor explained, though the hand was never going to move well, in fact it would hardly move at all, it was still there, almost in full, attached to the rest of me. "All four fingers and nails," he affirmed, as if there were nothing unusual about the number. He wrapped the gauze tightly around my hand as I glanced at the lifeless burden on the left side of my body.

Eventually, the nurse wheeled me into another room, away from the other victims of the explosion. She asked again if there was any-one else I wanted to call. "My husband," I repeated. Within minutes she returned to inform me that Muhsin still wasn't around. I sus-pected nothing. I knew he would come to me in time. Instead, I thought about my hand, about life with one functional hand instead of two. How much could that change a person's life? I could still dust, chop, caress. And Nasrin. How would she take it? It didn't matter then. I wouldn't be seeing her for a while.

When Muhsin finally appeared, he entered my hospital room with-out knocking. "Why did you go *there*?" he demanded in an accusatory tone, as though going to the post office carried the same implications as marching onto a battlefield. I didn't answer. The nurse had given me an injection, and my head grew heavy. I don't remember his leav-ing for the night. The next day Muhsin came in just as the nurse was changing the dressing on my wounds. He looked away as he spoke, focusing on the door instead of my hand. Evidently, the explosion had started a massive migration out of Tehran. When the nurse finished bandaging my hand, Muhsin rolled a television set into my room so I could watch for myself. As they aired scenes from the ex-plosion, I looked for glimpses of the young man lying beside me, but the reporter had moved on to another newsworthy event: a Tunisian caravan gone astray on the road to Damascus.

"You hear that?" I asked Muhsin.

He looked pale.

"I'm sorry," he said, putting his fingers through his greasy hair.

"Don't tell Nasrin."

"Okay," he said. "But what were you doing there?"

"Mailing her a letter."

As he spoke to me, Muhsin caressed my good hand, even though public displays of affection—even between married couples—were against the Islamic rules of the state-run hospital. I wanted him to stop but said nothing. Then, in one ugly second, I began to yank his hand, hoping to pull it out of socket as if it were an appendage on a doll. I yanked and yanked until Muhsin eventually shook me hard and told me to stop. Then he lit a cigarette and the smell of infirmity suffused the room. His eyes drifted away from my face and onto the white tiles beneath his feet.

"I was at work," he said quickly. "On site. It was Tuesday, remember?"

"Nasrin used to count tiles," I said.

"I came as soon as I heard."

"I guess she learned that from you."

As Muhsin reached for the pitcher to pour himself some water, his hands shook and he spilled the water on the floor. The second time he tried, the glass slipped out of his hands. Never before had an incident so alienated us. Not the revolution, the drugs, nor even Muhsin's short stays in prison, because none of it seemed as indelible as this. The knowledge of something good turned putrid bothered us, and my crippled hand displayed publicly the imperfection of our lives.

I knew then.

"Why you?" he whispered.

I felt him grope for my anger, but this time there was nothing. One who has lain next to death begins to hold onto life, however feebly.

"It's still in my purse," I told him.

"What?"

"The letter."

"I'll mail it myself," he offered, "and give some money to the poor."

"Please," I said. "Please take care of it."

"I will," he promised.

He never did.

Weeks later, I returned to the hospital to have the bandages removed from my hand. This time, Muhsin accompanied me throughout the ordeal, valiantly, as if instructed beforehand by the doctor. He didn't even cringe when he saw for the first time my twisted fingers and bent knuckles. I did. I wanted to rip my hand away, like a chicken bone, and dump it into a garbage bin, permanently out of sight.

"Try massaging it several times a day," the doctor said. "Soon you'll regain some feeling." He began rubbing my hand in soft vertical strokes and waited for me to take over. But when he released my hand, I let it drop to my side and instead watched a stray cat limp to the other side of the street from his office window. The doctor paused. "Like this," he offered again, taking my hand and exerting pressure upon it. He waited for me to imitate his motions, but without his encouragement the hand again fell to my side.

On the way out the doctor gave Muhsin a bag full of color-coded tubes. "This one numbs the pain; this one will heal the remaining cuts with minimal scarring; this one will . . ." I stopped listening to him, focusing only on the doctor's fourth finger. Would he have responded to his own pain in the same way that he reacted to the suffering of others?

The sun pierces the morning clouds as we drive to the doctor's office. Already, a long trail of outdated cars clogs the expressway. A driver to the left of us thrusts his head out the window to yell obscenities at a wayward pedestrian. Farther ahead, two cars stall abruptly, choking on leaded fuel, before chugging along. The car's irregular motion and frequent jerky halts make me dizzy. As I open a window to clear my head, noxious fumes waft inside the automobile, and I feel worse. "Close the window," Muhsin says. "The air is really dirty in this part of the city."

The doctor's office appears shortly after we turn onto Martyrdom Street. Since we were last here, fresh slogans have been painted on the concrete walls of the doctor's building. Muhsin begins reading some of them out loud: "A veil protects a woman's decency and prevents moral corruption." He lets out a loud, devilish laugh, and continues: "Death to the unveiled."

"Was that ever in the Qu'ran?" he asks.

I don't reply. It's the absence of opium that makes Muhsin moody. We enter the doctor's office and the nurse situates us in the waiting room. Muhsin picks up an old magazine, skims it, and loudly tosses it back on the table. Then, the doctor appears and directs us to the examination room. We smile politely and thank him for making time for us despite the short notice.

"Are you still using the medication?" he asks.

I nod. "But they don't stop the pain any more," I say.

Muhsin lights a cigarette and looks at the doctor.

"Go ahead," the doctor says to him.

As he exhales, a ripple of smoke spreads out, and I smell sickness again. Muhsin walks over to the window as the doctor gives me an injection. Before leaving, we make an appointment for the following month, and Muhsin asks if there's anything else we can do—a superfluous question he always feels compelled to pose. There is, of course, nothing more to do, and soon we are back on the expressway.

At the first red light Muhsin reaches over and takes my hand. He kisses it from the fingertips to the center of the palm. "This point here looks like a bird's nest," he says, referring to the corner where the life line and love line intersect. To me, the indentation looks more like a ditch.

"Don't go," I say.

Muhsin releases my hand, and his eyes wander from my wound to the window. I long to stare at him, into his eyes, but he twitches as the light turns green, and his eyes follow the morning traffic down Martyrdom Street and away from my sight.

⋈ PERSIS M. KARIM ⋈

Paris Rendez-vous

In some ways, my cousin's life and mine paralleled our fathers' lives. My father lived in America and her father lived in Iran. When her father was in prison under the Shah, mine was earning a respectable living and raising as normal a middle-class American family as an Iranian man and his French wife could. Uncle Antoine had been in prison for eight years under the Shah. Nearly three decades later, Minoo was in prison for almost five years for what was considered "counter-revolutionary activity." It seemed only a matter of chance that I was born an American and Minoo was born an Iranian. We had the same last name, and if the situation had been reversed, I suspect I, too, might have ended up in jail. Passion and idealism run deep in our family.

I'd been corresponding with Minoo since her release from jail in 1987. I didn't really know what to write to her then or even how to write to her—my Persian was poor and consisted only of a few phrases like "*halet chetoreh?*" "*dast-e-shoma dard nakonad,*" and "*aid-e shoma mobarak.*" What little else I knew was a smattering of romantic phrases I'd learned from the Gugush album (a popular female Iranian singer during the 1970s) my father brought home from his last trip to Iran in 1976—phrases like "*man o to*" and "*to ra dust daram.*" At that point, I'd started to study Persian and wrote the letters of the alphabet in the boxy stick-figure style of a child. After the obligatory salutations in Persian, "*salam, dokhtar amu-ye azizam*" (hello my dear cousin), the remainder of the letter proceeded in simple, straightforward English. I wanted her to understand. I had many questions and tried to ask them in ways that didn't overwhelm or offend. But my difficulty in writing was more than a simple language barrier. We were living worlds apart. Her teenage years had been filled with politics, demonstrations, and the tumult of a revolution. I, on the other hand, had been preoccupied with my studies and the social awkwardness of trying to fit in at a suburban American high school.

Minoo's English was a little better than my Persian. But not by much. Her education had been interrupted first by the revolution and then by a prison sentence handed down by the Islamic Republic. I tried to imagine her as a strong, but frightened, sixteen-year-old in a prison full of women who had set their sights on change; for them the revolution was the darkness of a cell and waiting, waiting for their lives to begin again. I couldn't imagine Minoo, who was only a few years younger than me, being swept up by the revolution, something I had never witnessed and would probably never see in my lifetime. Like so many others, she was a hopeful young person on the streets of Tehran demanding real change after decades of dictatorship and re-pression.

I never did learn the exact circumstances of her arrest. When we finally met in Paris, I was too afraid to ask. I could feel how much she wanted to escape the heaviness of her life and to simply forget that time. I was simply incapable of understanding how history could push itself through the seams of a person's life and tear it wide open. I had no idea who Minoo was before her time "in there" (as she used to call it in her letters), but I could feel the fragility of her life. It was a shadow that threatened to drown her in its silent shapes and tired edges. There was no language for that kind of pain.

When I came out of the Orly Airport terminal that cold February day in 1993, I recognized her immediately. She was far more beauti-ful in person than in the austere photos she had sent me several years earlier. She was dressed in a tight black sweater and black trousers and wore a long, fake leopard-skin coat—very glamourous and quite unlike the black-and-white photo she'd sent of herself in a black chador. Her eyes were big and beaming but with a hint of sadness that I recognized from the photos. Her round face and full lips were dramatic reminders of family features I had not inherited. It was a face that exuded soulfulness and a strange kind of peace I could only attribute to a person who's seen and lived too much, too early in life.

I had decided to meet Minoo in Paris because I couldn't get a visa to go to Iran. After some difficulty, she managed to get her passport reinstated and was finally free to travel abroad. She wanted to come to the United States on a tourist visa, and because our Uncle Jamshid had been sick and had had a double bypass operation, we thought this the prefect pretext for her visit. But it was far more important that she come for herself. Her life had never quite resumed its course. The idea of movement was more important than actually going somewhere. Prior to my arrival in Paris, she had gone to the U.S. embassy but had been denied a visa. No explanation was offered despite the fact that she had a job and a husband in Iran and had every intention of returning there after a visit to the States. Like all Iranians, she had the misfortune of coming from a country that had been declared a pariah state, a "terrorist nation." She'd saved for two years to make the journey to Paris, as she had been told that visas were more readily granted to Iranians in western cities than in the Middle Eastern capitals of Istanbul and Abu Dhabi. She called me from Paris to tell me the news, and I decided to meet her there to see if I could help. I wanted to meet the woman whose letters I had eagerly read for nearly six years.

I planned to spend only ten days with her, so I mapped out all the Parisian wonders I would take her to visit: the Louvre, the Jeu de Paume, Montmarte, Sacré-Coeur . . . I knew she was interested in art and photography, and I was determined to give her a whirlwind tour of Paris after we took care of business at the embassy. But we did none of this. When I asked her what she wanted to see and do, she told me she was interested in Paris cafés, in talking, and in just watching people go by. "But you're in Paris," I said. "Paris is the city of light, the city of artists, intellectuals, and exiles!" She looked at me with a sheepish grin and said, "All I want, dear cousin, is to drink wine, smoke cigarettes, and watch people, if you don't mind."

At first I didn't understand, but I soon did. The day after I arrived, we set out for the embassy but never made it to our destination. "Paris is beautiful," she would say, even though it was cold and gray. "There are so many different kinds of people." She was most fascinated by the Africans dressed in bright prints whom we had seen on the train. "Black people are so beautiful," she said. "I just want to kiss their lips." For her, the mélange of humanity, the bright colors were exhilarating. "In Tehran, everything is painted in shades of black," she said.

When we entered the subway at the Roosevelt station and descended the stairs, she pulled my arm gently. "Shhh, can you hear it?" she said in Persian. On the subway platform, a young Japanese man was playing a Bach suite on his cello, and despite the noise of passing trains and loudspeaker announcements, we could hear him quite well. A small crowd had gathered around him. Minoo was mesmerized. After several minutes our train went by. And another one and then another one. She was transfixed by the music, by the outbursts of expression, the traffic of people, the unbridled chaos, and the absence of spying eyes. "Shall we take the next train?" I asked after a few minutes. "Can we just sit and listen for a while?" she asked and gestured toward a bench. I resigned myself. Maps and plans were useless.

The next day we were determined to visit the U.S. embassy and make a second attempt at getting her a visa. This time, I would be her envoy. I was confident that they had rejected her because of her poor English and her passive demeanor. "I know how to handle these Americans," I told her, "after all, I'm one of them." If I could translate for her and convey our family solidarity, they would surely grant her a visa.

It was a cold and wet morning, and as we approached the building, my heart began to beat faster. I asked the guard seated at the entrance where the visa office was, and he gestured toward the glass door with a white-gloved hand. Although it was early, it seemed every other foreigner wanting to go to America was there. The attendant told us to fill out a form and wait in line.

I felt nervous and asked Minoo to tell me again what they had said to her. "Did they give you any indication of why they turned you down?" I asked. "No," she answered in English, "they didn't even look at my employment documents or my marriage certificate." I was puzzled. After about an hour of waiting, we were finally called. We approached the counter, and the tall, elegantly dressed woman behind the window asked us in a businesslike tone how she could help. Without thinking, I pulled out my American passport and showed her the cover. I explained Minoo's situation, that she was my cousin and that we were trying to get her to the United States to act as an emissary for our family in Iran since my uncle was sick in California. The woman refused to look at me and asked Minoo in a brusque tone, "Do you speak English?" "A little," she answered timidly. "Well, then, why don't you speak for yourself?" she asked.

I felt impatient and angry, but let Minoo explain her situation. She spoke slowly and softly. I wanted to shake her and tell her that dealing with American officials required a loud, confident voice. The woman looked at her passport again and asked several questions. "You live where? Why didn't you just go to an embassy closer to Iran? What do you want to do in the United States?" I nudged Minoo and whispered that she should show the woman her documents. She reluctantly pushed the documents through the metal slot below the window and said, "These are translations of my proof of employment and my marriage certificate." The woman picked them up and glanced at them quickly. "I'll be right back," she said. She went behind a door and we stood waiting for what seemed like twenty minutes. When she returned, she pushed the documents back through the slot of the counter toward Minoo. "I'm sorry Ms. Karim," she said, "you'll just have to apply for a visa closer to Tehran. We have no way of proving that this is your place of employment or that these documents are legitimate."

I couldn't hold my tongue.

"Look," I said impatiently, "my cousin came all this way, thinking you'd grant her a visa. She has all the documentation you need to give her a tourist visa. What's the problem?"

The woman gave me a blank stare and then, in a patronizing voice, turned toward Minoo and repeated her last statement adding that "it would be one thing if you were from Italy or even Yugoslavia, because we might be able to call there, but I have no way of confirming the legitimacy of these documents. I am sorry."

I butted in again, only this time I pushed my American passport under the window and began speaking. "As you can see, I am an American citizen, and I think you owe it to me to explain why you haven't even looked carefully at her documents."

The woman clearly had had it with me and with one quick gesture she pushed my passport back under the window. "I shouldn't have to explain anything to you," she said angrily. "You people are responsible for this situation. As an Iranian, you ought to know why we aren't letting Iranians into the country. It's not our fault the Iranian government has created this kind of tension."

I was dumbfounded. Wasn't there some protocol for decency? I butted in once again and pushed my open passport back through the slot so she could see my photo. "Can you please explain to me why you don't consider her documents legitimate? Is there some kind of unwritten policy that denies Iranians visas? If there is, why don't you just put up a sign?"

"I don't have to explain anything to you," she said as she closed my passport and pushed it back toward me. I spoke again and prefaced my comments by saying "as an American," believing that somehow those words would soften her attitude. "You should know that my cousin was a victim of her government," I said in a quivering but loud voice. "She was in prison under Khomeini. She's done nothing. All she wants is to visit her family in the States. Do you think she's a terrorist or something? She doesn't represent that government."

The woman's face grew red and without so much as looking in our direction said, "I'm sorry, I can't help you. Next in line please."

Minoo grabbed the corner of my jacket and pulled me out of the line. "Come on, *azizam*," she said, "it's hopeless. I knew they would turn me down."

I felt as if I had been kicked in the stomach. I looked into Minoo's eyes and began to cry. "I can't believe the way she treated us," I said. "She has no right to talk to us that way. We're not responsible for these stupid politics. Did you see how she lumped everyone together? They act like they're saviors, but they treat people like criminals."

Minoo pulled me close to her and held me in her arms. "Don't worry," she whispered while stroking my hair. "It's okay, I know how these things work. We tried."

Her resignation was like salt in my wound. I simply couldn't process it. Minoo was accustomed to abuses of power, to heartless bureaucracies, used to being turned away because of her passport. She knew better than anyone how governments make victims of their people. "What will you do?" I asked. "I'll go to Singapore," she said. "That's the only country that doesn't require a visa for Iranians. I'll try to go to the university there." I felt sorry for Minoo, but even sorrier for myself.

The day before I left Paris it rained heavily. A cold, hard rain. We had decided to try to get a copy of her father's French birth certificate to see if with his documents we could secure a French visa for her. It would take some time, but I could at least help Minoo get the process started. We knew the approximate date of her father's birth, but because his birth certificate had been lost, no one knew for sure. Both of our fathers had been born in Paris, and because I knew my father's birthdate and had a copy of our grandmother's *carte de séjour* (residency papers) with the names of her two French-born sons on it, I thought it wouldn't be too difficult to locate her father's birth certificate. My uncle was born three years earlier than my father, and both had been born in the sixth arrondissement of Paris in a Catholic hospital. That, my father had told me, explained why they both had Christian names.

We made our way to the *mairie* (district office) in the sixth arrondissement and found the office that maintains records of births, deaths, and property titles. Although my French wasn't fluent, I managed to convey that we needed to obtain a copy of a birth certificate. I unfolded the copy of my grandmother's residency papers and tried to explain to the woman behind the desk that we needed this birth certificate because my uncle had lost his many years ago in Iran and had never bothered to have it replaced. "What's the name, date of birth, father's name?" she asked. "His name's Antoine Karim," I said. "I don't know the exact date of birth, 1913 I think, September maybe. But I know his father's name. Mumtaz Abdul-Karim. After all, how many Iranians could have been born in Paris in 1913?" I asked rhetorically. She laughed and shrugged her shoulders.

The woman busily fingered through her bound books of birth certificates in front of us. She looked up my grandfather's name and then my grandmother's name, but found nothing.

"Are you certain he was born in this arrondissement?" she asked.

"All I know is he was born in a Catholic hospital and they lived here in the sixth."

"Ah, well," she said. "You'll have to go to the district where he was born. There's no Catholic hospital here. Go to the *mairie* in the eighth or the eleventh."

We took our umbrellas and walked to the subway and eventually made it to the *mairie* in the eighth arrondissement. I explained what we wanted to the woman at the front desk, and I handed her the copy of my grandmother's papers.

"Okay, now," she said, "let me get this straight. The two of you have fathers who were born in Paris, neither of them lives here, neither one of you lives here, and you're Iranian and you're American," she said pointing to us in succession. "And why do you want this birth certificate?"

"As a souvenir of our *rendez-vous*," I said in my imperfect French. "We're paying homage to the place where our fathers began their lives."

Although she was reluctant to help, she must have been convinced, because she went to the back office and emerged a few minutes later saying that she had found someone named Marie Abdul-Karim but not Maryam—the name I had given her. "That's her!" I said, "that's my grandmother. I'm certain they Frenchified her name."

"Well," the woman continued, "there is an Antoine Abdul-Karim, but you have the wrong date and year for his birth. This one was born in 1912 in November."

"That's him!" I said eagerly. "I'm sure of it."

The woman shook her head and laughed. "It's a little confused, your family," she said in English. Then in French she explained that in order for Minoo to get a copy of the birth certificate, she would have to prove that she was, in fact, this Antoine's daughter. "She has a translated copy of her passport," I said. "Show her, Minoo."

The translation, however, was not in French; in order to get the birth certificate we would have to obtain an official French translation. The woman pointed to a translation and notary service down the street.

"And anyway," she said, "her name is Karim, not Abdul-Karim. How can I release a copy to you?"

I explained to her that we were both Karims, that our grandfather had dropped the "Abdul" when he lived in France, and no longer used it in Iran because he didn't like the implications of being *abdul*—"a slave of god." "Look," I said, "look at my passport. I am Karim, too. We're cousins, I swear. My father is Alexandre, I am his daughter, see it's in my passport."

I felt discouraged again. How could we make these institutions understand the traces of travel and movement within our family that a document couldn't register? "My father and her father were born here, but they went back to Iran after the First World War," I explained. "My father eventually emigrated to America, and I was born there. My mother, in fact, is French," I said throwing in another detail to confuse her.

Now the woman looked even more puzzled. "Let me get this straight, you're American, she's Iranian, and your fathers were both born in Paris? And you have a French mother?"

"Yes," I said, "That's right."

It seemed simple enough to us.

"Well," she said smiling, "I appreciate your complexity but you still have to prove to me that she is Antoine's daughter. I will need a French translation."

"Please, please," I pleaded. "This was such a long trip for my cousin, and all we want is this one souvenir of our meeting. I'm leaving tomorrow morning, and all we want is a copy. Not even the original, please? Can't you just give it to us? We've been through enough hassles with bureaucracies, and all we want is this little piece of paper."

My begging worked. She left the room and came back a few minutes later with the copy in hand. "Don't tell anyone," she said holding her index finger against her lips. "I could lose my job."

"Thank you so much," I said. "Of course, we won't tell a soul."

On the way back to the apartment where we were staying, we saw the newspaper headlines in the afternoon edition of *Le Monde*. The United Nations building in New York had been bombed, hundreds were injured, and several people had been killed. "*Qui sont les terroristes?*" read the headlines. There was, of course, immediate speculation that Iranians had been involved.

"This will make it harder for me to go anywhere," Minoo said in a defeated tone. "We carry the weight of the world's anger on our shoulders."

I didn't know what to say. We rode the train home in silence. After several minutes, I grabbed Minoo's hand and held it tight inside mine. "We'll find a way to get you somewhere, even if not to the U.S." I said in a falsely reassuring voice. I had no idea what to do or say. I had no idea what she must be feeling. All I knew was that by the time I left my cousin in Paris the following day, nations and their documents were senseless pieces of paper. My American passport had meant nothing and Minoo's Iranian passport had meant everything.

Ed McMahon Is Iranian

It was a typical afternoon. My mother and I were spending time together arranging things in our new Florida home while my little brother was napping.

Then the doorbell rang. As my mom opened the door, a huge explosion occurred. BANG!

With the explosion came a splash of red paint that stained our front door. The scarlet stains on the door branded us: terrorists. My mom slammed the door shut and immediately called my father at work. All I remember is being scared and not knowing what had happened. I could sense that my mom was terrified, which scared me even more. She tried to reassure me that everything was all right and asked me to go to my room and take a nap. Then the police arrived, and she told them what had happened.

That night when Dad came home, I didn't know what to ask him or what to say; there was an uncomfortable silence and an unspoken tension in the air. After dinner I approached my dad. I curled up next to him in his big brown leather seat, which had become imprinted with the shape of his back.

"So, Daddy, who did that thing today?"

My father looked to my mom for help in answering, but she remained quiet. I could tell that he was scrambling for a suitable answer for his curious five-year-old daughter. "Vell, someone deed dis because dey vere mad at the Eraniyans who var holding fifty-two American hostages."

"Mad at us? We didn't do anything? Did we?"

"No, ve did not, but dey tink it is our fault."

"I hate being Iranian. I'm not going to make any friends at my new school because they will all hate me. They will always hate me. I don't want to be Iranian. No one I know is Iranian. I wish I were American."

I was sad and petrified at the same time.

"You are an American, Maryam. You vere born in dis country."

"No, I wish I were a *real* American. No one here is an Iranian."

My parents looked at each other for a painful second, then my dad looked up at the television—the *Tonight Show with Johnny Carson* was on—desperate for an answer to my bold declaration. "You are wrong," he suddenly blurted out. "Dere are many Eraniyans in de USA."

I looked up at him skeptically. "Like who?" I asked.

Then he pointed to the fat man on the screen. "Heem, Ed Mac MA Hohn is Eraniyan."

Through my tears, I looked at the fat man on the TV. Him? He was an Iranian? Call it naïveté or just childhood ignorance, or maybe it was the fact that I needed to believe my father—whatever it was, I let myself believe it. Of course my dad, with his accent, could have made John F. Kennedy sound like an Iranian name, but that didn't matter to me.

For years I honestly believed that Ed McMahon was Iranian. I would tell my friends, my brothers, everyone, that Ed was Iranian. Every time one of those sweepstakes letters came in the mail, I thought Ed had sent it to us because he knew we were Iranians, too. Of course, every time Ed was on television my dad would say: "Look, dere's Ed Mac MA Hohn, he's Eraniyan."

Now, eighteen years later, Ed Mac MA Hohn is a little joke in our house. My dad still likes to "Iranianize" names of celebrities and try to "trick" us, and I still like to let him do it.

⤳ NIKA KHANJANI ⤶

The Eyebrow

"Here. Suck this."

My brother, a sympathetic eight-year-old, stretches out his hand, which holds a dripping cherry popsicle, hoping it will pacify my cries and squeals. Through my tears and the needle-like pricks in the space where my eyebrows used to flair, I see my mother's concentrated face. Her eyes are wide and focus on the enemy. Her own eyebrows are tamed to thin, perfect arches after years of pruning.

"Aaah! Ooww! STOP! Mom, it hurts!"

"*Vool nakon,* Nika *jan,*" she says. "Almost over."

But it seems that she's been plucking that damn left brow for hours. I won't do this to my daughter, I swear. She can run around with grass-stained jeans and wild eyebrows until she's eighty-seven. And she'll never feel bad.

I search the kitchen for something to distract me from this torture. The heavy smell of dried lemon simmering in the *khoresh* (stew). A steady cloud of steam is coming off the towel on the rice pot. I imagine the adults at tonight's dinner party. They'll glance at each other and nod in approval. "*Bah, bah! Cheqad khub!* How delicious!" they will say, as always.

Mom's cooking is famous. Friends forget about *ta'rofing* when she invites them over for dinner. No one will miss out tonight, especially since she's making her delicious rice with the golden *tadiq* (the crunchy rice at the bottom of the pan).

But my neck is cramping and my back hurts from sitting on this metal fold-up chair that guests never use—only us.

"Oww, Mom, hurry up! This is killing me! I'll be the only dead fifteen-year-old with perfect eyebrows."

"I know, I know, Nika *jan*." But her eyes stay fixed as though she's stitching a head injury. "Almost done."

I feel the hairs fall on my face, my nose, and my lips. It itches like crazy. Sometimes Mom can read my mind. She uses the hand with the tweezers to brush the fallen hairs away. These are the same old tweezers she uses to do her own eyebrows only she *never* flinches. I will never get used to this. My eyebrows are much too stubborn, each hair unwillingly pulled out one by one. They put up a fight. So do I. My arms flail and I finally bolt from the chair.

"Nika, you can't go like that! You only have one eyebrow finished. You look ridiculous!"

"I don't care."

"Nika, you are a woman now. You have to refine the way you look. Come and let me finish the other one."

"I'm no woman! Look at me—I have the curves of a celery stick! And since when do eyebrows have anything to do with being a woman?" I knew what she meant, though. In order to join the circle of other Iranian women, I had to do it. It was my rite of passage. And she understood my reluctance.

She stands, looks at me, and laughs. Even though I'm frustrated and embarrassed, I can't help but smile. She hands me the mirror to see what I've endured. And there it is. My sign of womanhood. Not bad.

"See, like a nice frame for your eye," she says as I compare it to the other one that hasn't been tamed . . . yet.

The Bricklayer

It all looked like the fragments of a shattered dream: the dusk, the dark indigo sky, and the way the airport minibus drove over an end-less road at what seemed to be the speed of light. He craned his neck, but couldn't see the driver. It was as if the bus drove itself. Sitting on the slippery edge of his seat, he clawed the front seat and ignored his twin daughters who sat on either side of him. They looked at him lov-ingly while they studied his aged face. His daughters hadn't seen him for many years.

Could all this be true? It was more like one of his recurring night-mares: a remote land with long roads, fast-moving cars, tall build-ings, dark corridors, and elevators that always got stuck between floors. Now the bus drove through a crooked street, making several right and left turns before it finally stopped.

The girls helped him out of the car, held his arms, and walked him through a sand-covered courtyard to a basement. It was dark every-where. He couldn't see, but he could hear the sound of a chain clink-ing. He wanted to remove the eye patch from his bad eye, but his daughters held his arms tightly. He couldn't speak. Once inside the basement, they guided him onto a doorless elevator. Someone pushed a button and the metal box squeaked, then groaned, and finally took them up to the house. He wasn't even sure whose house this strange place was. Did it belong to Abi, the daughter who was a teacher and had a husband, or Bibi, the other one, who didn't have a job and was divorced? It didn't matter. All he needed was to be alone, to remove his eye patch, and to let the light in. He had to let the light inside his head.

So, this was America. And this place was where he had to stay "for a little while," which was what they were telling him, until his son-in-law could find him and his wife a house. "A house," he murmured—then he said, "home" and repeated the word so many times it lost its meaning.

"Home, home, home, home," he murmured, moving from one room to another and peering through all six windows of his daughter's house. He stood at the bedroom window, looking at the neighbor's yard and the cracked roof that seemed as if it were sinking, almost falling on the black man's head. In the middle of the yard was a big, yellow bathtub that had pieces of its enamel chipped off. The neighbor used the tub to collect rain water. Why? the old man wondered, but didn't want to think hard to find the answer. He stood in front of the kitchen window and looked at his daughter's yard: a big sand-covered space, with only one small flower-bed on the left. The dark fresh soil indicated that the bed had been recently, but hastily planted. Now the dog was digging up the pansies. Mr. Parvin peered from another window and noticed a bar with blinking red neon lights in its window. Some disheveled-looking men went in and out of the bar. Where exactly was this house? he wondered. Was his daughter poor? He looked around to see if anyone was nearby so he could remove the eye patch. But his wife sat close-by unpacking the suitcases. She took out their son's framed picture, lay it in front of her on the table, and then started to fold and unfold clothes.

Mr. Parvin sat down at the kitchen table to eat. His daughters, Abi and Bibi, kissed his cheeks. In a flash of memory he remembered them as two little girls, sitting on his lap; one on his right leg, the other on his left. He remembered the scent of their hair, too, sweet and grassy at the same time. But he didn't want to remember anything more. All he wanted was to be left alone, and they wouldn't let him be. What if they wouldn't give him a chance to be alone? What if they'd hover about him all the time? Now they were talking about finding a place, a house. His son-in-law was going to show them a house with a yard, so that Mr. Parvin could sit on a bench and look at the plants. "House," he said, smiled, and bent his head low on the plate, almost touching the food with the tip of his nose. He ate as fast as he could, making munching and gulping sounds. He felt everyone's gaze on him. His wife's burning eyes pierced his head. He raised his eyes. She motioned to him to lift his head and eat properly. He smiled and this time lifted the spoon so slowly that midway the soup spilled out. One of his daughters burst into tears, mumbling between sobs, loudly, hysterically, the way she used to cry and mumble when she was little, upsetting everybody. It was Bibi.

"What's . . . happened . . . to *Baba?*" she asked between hiccups.

Living in his daughter's house "for a little while" seemed like an eternity. So where was this house his son-in-law was going to show them? When his wife scrubbed his back in the bathtub he whispered, "the house," and she whispered back, "soon, soon." He didn't say anything; he just touched his black eye-patch with his wet fingers, as if wanting to remove it. His wife told him not to touch it. Then he sat motionless and let her remove it and shampoo his hair. Thick, white hair; a mass of useless hair. He now vaguely remembered himself with his thick black hair, combed back and set with Vaseline. But he didn't want to remember anything more. He listened to the hollow sounds of the bathroom. His wife's heavy breathing, gasping almost, toiling to wash the heavy bulk of his body and his thick white mane. Through the curtain of water covering his face he glanced at the bathroom window with his good eye. His bad eye was shut tight. He was tempted to open it and let the light in, let the colors happen, and let the bricklayer come. But he didn't; he kept the bad eye closed, and his wife covered it with the patch again.

Since that first day he avoided the doorless elevator. His son-in-law insisted that he use it to go down to the yard—it was safe. He was an engineer and had designed and built the elevator just for Mr. Parvin, so that he wouldn't have to use the narrow steps. But the old man avoided the squeaky elevator. What if it stopped between the first floor and the basement, in the middle of the dark? He used the narrow stairway instead and took one step after another. Holding onto the cold wall, he placed his good foot first, dragged his bad foot behind, and secured it next to the good one. It took him forever to get to the yard. He thought he'd lost most of his morning and felt irritated. Mornings were when everybody finally went to work and his wife became busy with cooking and left him alone for a little while.

At last he was in the yard; he could enjoy himself. First he made sure that Gorgi, the huge gray dog was chained up. Then he limped up and down the yard several times, listening to the crackling of the sand under his shoes. He glanced at Gorgi repeatedly to make sure he was asleep, or resting his head on his paws, watching him with sad eyes. He counted his trips to the gate and back to the steps—ten. Then he sat on the steps and looked at the flower bed. He noticed new flowers in the place where Gorgi had dug up the old pansies. He loved pansies. He always used to have them in his yards back home; maybe that was why his daughter had planted them. But he didn't want to think about the pansies or his daughter. He just watched the blossoms without feeling anything. They were carefully chosen. The colors were dark and light shades of blue-purple and the lavender of dusk. The large but fragile blossoms bent under their own weight, as if a row of shy girls stood in front of him, posing self-consciously. But enough of them, he thought. His precious morning was passing by. His wife would call him any minute to go up and have lunch.

He was alone, the sun was in the sky, and Gorgi was asleep. Now he could remove the eye patch, and his guest would appear. But first the lights would come. Back home, the doctor had explained that these lights and images appeared because of his torn retina. The light hit this crack, creating many colorful shapes. He had a kaleidoscope in his eye, and he could entertain himself any time he wanted. Just by sitting in the sun and removing the eye patch he could see a whole other world. When his wife first saw him doing this she scolded him for damaging his eye even more. But then she left him alone. She didn't know about the rest though. No one knew about the bricklayer who visited Mr. Parvin.

He was simply called "the bricklayer." He had no other name. He came into Mr. Parvin's life after he acquired the kaleidoscope, after he began speaking less and less. The bricklayer was a man in his forties with a sun-baked face, a deeply creased forehead, dark piercing eyes, and wide brown hands with clay and mortar dried on them. He was broad shouldered. A real worker.

"Good morning, my friend!"

"Good morning, Mr. Parvin!" the bricklayer said.

"Sit here, on these steps."

"Thank you, Mr. Parvin."

"What's going on at home?"

"The same, sir. They're arresting more and more people and locking them up."

"Even the old people?"

"Even the old ones like yourself."

"They arrested me once."

"I know. Don't I?"

Mr. Parvin sighed and continued to sit with the bricklayer, saying nothing. His visits with the worker were always like this. Relaxed and informal. Neither of them forced the other one to talk. They talked only if there was a need. Now, he wasn't thinking about the prison or the prisoners. He didn't want to. Gazing at the pansies, relaxing, he simply felt good and safe. His friend was next to him.

At the dinner table that evening, his family sat around him, all talking at the same time, when suddenly Mr. Parvin slammed his knife on his plate and made them quiet. For a second, the shrieking voices of his daughters echoed in the silent kitchen, and when everybody was finally quiet, he stood up. Behind him the kitchen window framed the orange glow of the fall sunset. Everybody stared at him at the head of the table. He could hear his wife's heart and saw the blue vein on her temple throbbing with anxiety. What was he going to say? He hadn't spoken a full sentence since they'd arrived; only a few scattered words came out of his mouth now and then. His daughters had actually thought that their father had lost his speech after the stroke.

"Grandpa wants to talk!" his little red-haired granddaughter said, breaking the silence. The freckle-faced girl was Abi's daughter and Mr. Parvin had avoided her since he'd arrived. Someone hushed her now, and he listened to the silence again. Gorgi rolled on the sand, and the sound of his chain rattling could be heard. It was a sound that made Mr. Parvin remember why he hit his knife against his plate in the first place. He had to tell them the truth. He had to tell his daughters everything.

"They took me there," he said. "Back home. They hit me with that heavy book, on my head. The man said, 'Are you trying to become a hero, old man?' I said, 'No, sir!' Then they hit me with the book again. Here, let me show you!"

He rubbed the right side of his head, and his daughters immediately got up and rushed to him. They took turns touching the spot just as they had when they were little, when they would sit on his lap and play with his hair. The two alternately rubbed the bump, which felt like a hard walnut, softly under their fingers.

"They didn't hit him," his wife said calmly, "he always had that bump. When he was a kid he fell from a tree or a wall or something," she said.

"They took me to the dark room," Mr. Parvin continued, still standing against the window. "They asked me where my son was. I said, 'My son is here, with you!'"

"What is all this about, *Maman?*" Bibi burst out.

"Why haven't you told us about this?" Abi echoed.

"After your brother escaped, they arrested your father," Mrs. Parvin said. "It was just a brief interrogation. They wanted to know where your brother was. That's all."

"They beat him!" Bibi said, sobbing loudly.

"With a heavy book! Here!" Mr. Parvin added.

"He is making this part up. They didn't hit him," Mrs. Parvin insisted.

"But his retina was torn," Abi said and wiped her eyes.

"That was six months later," Mrs. Parvin explained. "Your brother was hiding for six months. Finally, they found him and locked him up. Your father had the stroke after he heard the news. The stroke did this to him, damaged the right side of his body and his right eye."

Now Mrs. Parvin was weeping into her napkin. "What a nightmare I went through. My son being tortured, my husband paralyzed, and none of you there to help me."

"With a heavy book," Mr. Parvin repeated. "And the man said, 'Are you trying to become a hero, old man?'"

The twins took their parents to the bedroom, gave them each a tranquilizer, and sat in the living room with the television on, but with no volume so that it was quiet. It was raining outside. They could hear the water pouring into the neighbor's bathtub. Sometimes a drunk sailor sang, coming out of the bar; sometimes Gorgi, now wet and impatient, shook himself, clattering his chain. The sisters sat there through the long hours of the night, even after the red-haired girl and her father went to bed. They lit a candle in front of their brother's picture, remembering him in silence.

Mr. Parvin didn't mind anymore if Gorgi sat at his feet, rubbing his wet muzzle on his pants. He said a few words to him and then removed the eye patch. When he looked around the yard with his eyes open he felt anxious. What if it didn't happen this time? He talked about this with Gorgi.

"Gorgi Khan, I'm going to cover my good eye and uncover my bad eye. Do you know what that means? It means that the lights and colors will come in. Ah . . . I'm covering the damn bastard. Oh, Gorgi, poor dog, I'm sorry for you. All you can see with your doggy eyes is black and white, isn't it? Do you know what I'm seeing? Hundreds of diamonds, circles, triangles, and nameless shapes in hundreds of colors. It's unbelievable! He is coming now. He is pushing the shapes aside and getting closer to me. You have to leave me Mr. Gorgi; go, my friend, make some space for my guest!" He pushed the dog, and when the dog didn't move, he nudged him gently with the tip of his shoe. The bricklayer sat where the dog was sitting before, and Mr. Parvin felt excited, overjoyed.

"You're here again, my friend. Welcome!"

"I'm here all right, Mr. Parvin. I'm here whenever you really want to see me."

"That's good. Very good. I'm not alone. You are my companion. My comrade. Now tell me about home. What's new?"

"Nothing is new, sir. All is the same. Yesterday they stoned a man and a woman in a marketplace. They buried them up to their waists so that they wouldn't be able to run away. They stoned them to death."

"What's happening in prison?"

"Executions. Every day."

"Early mornings, huh?"

"Any time now. At sunset, too."

"How are they? The boys and the girls?"

"They are heroic, Mr. Parvin. They sing up until the last minute."

"Did he sing, too?"

"He sang."

"You're saying this to make me happy, huh?"

"No. I was there, sir. He sang."

That evening at the table Mr. Parvin hit his knife on the plate again, making another brief speech. He told his daughters how the author-ities executed their brother. He described the whole scene as if he had been there and witnessed it.

"Around five o'clock they blindfolded them, took them out of their cells. They walked them through the long corridors and led them to a big hall. There the boys waited on their feet for a long time. In the dark. That's when your brother started to sing."

"Okay, that's enough now!" Mrs. Parvin dropped her spoon.

"No, it's not enough. There's a lot more," Mr. Parvin said and con-tinued. "Do you know what he sang? 'From the blood of our youth tulips are growing, tulips are growing, tulips are growing . . .'" He raised his voice, singing out of tune.

Bibi rushed to the bathroom. Everybody heard her sobbing vio-lently, coughing, then throwing up. Her sister followed her.

"Sit down now," Mrs. Parvin said. "You ruined dinner. Eat!"

"But I haven't told the rest of the story."

"No one wants to hear it. It's all in your head. No one was there to know how it happened."

"I have a source there. I trust him." He said this, and immediately he regretted it. He shouldn't have said anything about the brick-layer.

Everybody left the table. He could hear them arguing in the other room. At first it was a quarrel between the mother and the girls. Then they started to shout at each other. The girls blamed their mother for withholding information about their father and brother. Then something broke. The little girl cried and rushed to the kitchen where Mr. Parvin sat alone against the dark window. He spoke to her for the first time, asking her her name.

"Do you know me?"

"You're Grandpa," the girl said, still crying, rubbing her eyes.

"And who are you?"

"I'm Sharah."

"Sharah or Sarah?"

"Sharah," the girl said firmly.

"Can I call you Shahrzade?"

"Okay."

Sharah's father came and took her to bed. Mr. Parvin stepped out to the porch. Holding his right hand against the wall, he descended the steps down to the dark yard. He sat on the last step for a long time with Gorgi lying at his side. He didn't talk to the dog but listened to his breathing, smelled his woolen smell, and felt his warmth. It was too dark to see anything, but he could feel the pansies not far from him dropping their heads, giving out a faint sweet scent.

There was a family meeting late that night. Mr. Parvin's son-in-law was trying to find a "logical solution" for everything. The old man could hear them from behind the wall of the bedroom. Although they had given him a pill, he couldn't sleep. He could also hear the black neighbor in his yard moving the old bathtub, which was making a scraping sound.

"I've made an appointment for his eyes," Mr. Parvin's son-in-law was saying. "After the surgery the house will be ready."

"You may fix up his eyes, but what about his brain? He's gone insane!" Mrs. Parvin said, weeping.

"He is not insane, *Maman*. We have to let him talk. Why do you shut him up?" one of the girls asked.

Mr. Parvin heard his wife answering and the sisters talking back at the same time. Things became confused again. They raised their voices, and the little girl suddenly burst into tears. Mr. Parvin pulled the blanket over his head to muffle the sounds. But then he heard the bedroom door bang, and his wife came in. He pretended to be asleep and from under the blanket saw her standing in front of the bathroom mirror wiping away her tears. She was tall and skeletal, a bit stooped, and she had started to shrivel—the way old people do when it seems they lose their bone tissue. Mr. Parvin remembered his wife as a young and beautiful woman. She never wore high heels to avoid looking awkward standing next to her shorter husband. She was still crying in front of mirrors—an old habit. Mr. Parvin remembered her crying in front of many mirrors when she was young. She cried whenever something went wrong. Their daughters became crybabies, too, and now little Sharah was crying her lungs out in the other room.

"Cry, cry! Let's all cry!" Mr. Parvin threw off the blanket and sat up in the bed. His long white hair was disheveled. His pajama buttons were open, revealing his old red skin creasing at his neck and chest like the spongy skin of a rooster's double chin. Bibi ran in, sat on the bed, and hugged her father tightly. She wept on his shoulder. She was the dramatic one. Abi, who was carrying her crying daughter in her arms, rushed to the bathroom to embrace her mother. The son-in-law stood under the frame of the door and watched the Parvin family. He, too, wiped his tears.

The man next door had pulled his broken chair close to the bath-tub and sat next to it as if he were sitting by a pool. He opened a can of beer and began singing a sailor's song with an accent Mr. Parvin could not understand or identify. But the song was so sad that it made the old man weep in his daughter's arms.

"Where is this place you're living, huh? Is this really America or is your husband poor?"

"I don't have a husband, *Baba*. This is Abi's house. I'm just staying here—temporarily."

"Is your sister poor?"

"This is the only place we could afford, *Baba*," the son-in-law said. "I'm an engineer, but I'm making keys in the corner of a grocery store. We've been trying to save some money to move to a better neighbor-hood. But now we have to think about your home, sir. This is our pri-ority."

"Home," Mr. Parvin said and sighed.

The next day, while sitting on the last step of the porch, in front of the pansies and next to Gorgi and with Sharah on his lap, Mr. Parvin told the bricklayer about the events of the night before. The brick-layer repeated the word "surgery" several times.

"Why do you repeat this word, my friend? You don't mean to tell me . . ."

"It's all up to you, sir. See if you can avoid the surgery. But if you can't, then I may be able to come, or I may not. It's going to be harder. Much harder."

"I want your company, bricklayer. And it's not just because you bring me news. I like you, my friend. You're wise."

"I have to go now. There is a wall I have to finish back home."

"May I ask whose house you're building?"

"It's a new penitentiary, sir. I'm raising the walls."

"What an awful job, bricklayer. Couldn't you say no?"

"If I'd say no, they would put me inside the walls."

"I understand."

For a few days Mr. Parvin couldn't call the bricklayer. It rained day and night, the basement flooded, and he heard his son-in-law walking with rubber boots knee-deep in the water, trying to sweep the flood out. The old man sat most of the day by the kitchen window, watching the gate. Gorgi was in the flooded basement. Mr. Parvin wondered how the poor dog could lie down. He thought about the surgery and what the bricklayer had told him. "See if you can avoid it." How could he avoid it? They would take him by force. He fantasized about escaping, going somewhere his family couldn't find him. He daydreamed about a sunny place, where he could freely remove the eye patch and call his friend.

It rained and rained and rained. Mr. Parvin's wife ironed, cooked quietly, now and then glanced at their son's picture, and sniffled. Bibi, the jobless twin, locked herself up with a migraine headache and Abi went to school in tall rubber boots and a long raincoat, returning later with wet grocery bags and bringing news about the flood. Sharah was in and out of the kitchen all day, hugging a bald doll or licking a lollipop. Sometimes she sat on her grandfather's lap. Mr. Parvin whispered into her ear, "Are you my Shahrzade?" She nodded. "Tell me a story, then," he said, and Sharah would shrug her shoulders and leave Mr. Parvin's lap to wander about the house.

"Rain, rain, rain . . ." Mr. Parvin muttered and vaguely recalled the many sunny days back home when his children played in the yard, and he watched them through the window, feeling proud of himself. He was a history teacher, wrote articles now and then, published here and there. But watching his children in the sun, he bragged to his scholar friends, "My best works, my masterpieces, are my children!"

A gust of wind opened the yard's gate and, like the scene of a foggy, half-forgotten dream, Gorgi ran toward the gate and left. He whispered, "Gorgi!" but no one heard him. Since his last speech at the dinner table he hadn't spoken much, and it was difficult to make the effort to speak. He struggled to raise himself from his chair using the table and chairs, then the walls and doorknobs to steady himself. At last he dragged himself to the room where his wife was ironing sheets and pillowcases. He whispered, "Gorgi," but his wife didn't pay attention.

Mr. Parvin heard the squeaky elevator. His son-in-law came up all wet, with water dripping from his hair and eyeglasses. The old man said, "Gorgi!" several times, motioning to the gate. His son-in-law rushed back inside the elevator and down to the yard.

"My head! My head is bursting! Please don't run that damned elevator!" Bibi banged her head on the wall. She was sitting on a cot, wearing a black scarf around her forehead and had eyes like a pirate.

Which of my daughters are you? he wanted to ask. But he didn't or couldn't. He guessed this must be the homeless one, the jobless one, the one without a husband. He tried to remember who had been her husband and what happened to him, but he couldn't concentrate and soon forgot about it. Limping to the bathroom, he closed the door and turned the lights on. There were eight bulbs around the mirror; he stared at them and removed the eye patch. Light poured inside his head. Closing his good eye tightly, he looked at the colorful shapes. He blinked, and the shapes changed form and became something else. From behind the red and purple diamonds, the bricklayer emerged; first, as a midget, then growing taller, and finally becoming the size of a tall man. Mr. Parvin put down the toilet lid and motioned to the bricklayer to sit down.

"Sorry, friend. We can't go out. Sit on this. My wife has cleaned it.
How are you?"

"As good as I can be."

"Something wrong?"

"The same."

"How is the wall?"

"The wall is rising. I'm working on it."

Mr. Parvin sighed and said nothing.

The bricklayer looked very gloomy and rubbed his face as if he was
tired. "When is your surgery?" he asked in a matter-of-fact way.

"The surgery? Oh, the eye surgery. One of these days. Should I be
worried?"

"They're going to sew up your retina, you'll be able to see with your
right eye."

"No colors and shapes?"

"No."

"And you?"

"It all depends. We'll see. Now I must go." The bricklayer stood up,
stretched his long body, and peered through the window. "A nasty
place, isn't it? Look at your neighbor down there. His umbrella is full
of holes. Is he crazy?"

"He is not the only crazy one around here, my friend. I'll see you on
the first sunny day. Bye."

Turning the lights out, Mr. Parvin stepped into the bedroom. His
wife sat on the edge of the bed staring at the bathroom door. Her eyes
were wet.

"I . . . was washing my hands . . . ," he mumbled.

"I know. Come, let me comb your hair."

She sat him down at the dressing table and began combing his thick
white hair. She did it gently, tenderly, as if she were still in love with
him. She ran the comb through his hair slowly, taking her time, pro-

longing it. She didn't put anything on her husband's hair. She liked the soft, silky feel of it.

"Did you hear me in the bathroom?" Mr. Parvin asked guiltily.

"No, dear, I didn't," she said in a whisper.

Mr. Parvin's son-in-law didn't come home until eleven that night. His dinner had become cold, and his wife walked back and forth restlessly, chewing her nails. Sharah burst into tears every fifteen minutes. Pressing his forehead against the cold windowpane, Mr. Parvin curved his hands around his face to see into the dark yard. Finally his son-in-law entered the open gate, dragging a heavy sack on the ground. The twins wore identical raincoats, made of shiny yellow rubber, and rushed to the yard. Mr. Parvin saw them taking Gorgi's corpse out of the burlap sack. The neighbor appeared with a shovel. It was pouring as if the sky were an upside-down sea. Mr. Parvin had to make an effort to see what they were doing.

What he saw seemed like fragments from a nightmare: the black man digging a grave along the wall of the yard, Mr. Parvin's daughters and his son-in-law lifting the heavy dead body of a dog, dumping it into the hole, and covering it with wet mud. In a minute they came up on the doorless elevator, muddy from head to foot, bringing the neighbor with them to the kitchen to eat. The girls sobbed, blowing their noses. Gorgi had been their companion since their first days in America. The neighbor said something no one understood. He shook his head in regret. The son-in-law opened a can of beer for him. Mrs. Parvin fed him some warm soup.

It rained for one more week, and when they sat at the kitchen table or in the living room they heard the tides of the flood water hitting the walls of the basement. Mr. Parvin's son-in-law gave up on sweeping out the rain water. He sat all day, pulling the prickly hairs of his thick moustache, thinking about a logical solution to the mess. The schools were all closed. Abi, the teacher, didn't go out anymore. The twins sat in front of the silent television, watching the maps and charts of the weather channel. Most of the week, Mr. Parvin limped the length of the house from one window to another, waiting for the rain to stop. He had been standing at the bedroom window for a few seconds when the black neighbor raised his head and waved to him. Mr. Parvin waved back. The neighbor sat on a broken chair next to his overflowing bathtub, holding a crooked umbrella over his head. He was drinking a beer.

On the first dry day, Mrs. Parvin combed her husband's hair back and splashed some cologne on his face. She wore her good dress—the black crepe skirt and jacket she wore when she arrived in this country. She put on some lipstick. The twins dressed up, and little Sharah wore a big pink bow on top of her red curls. They all crammed into Abi's small Toyota to take Mr. Parvin to the hospital. Although the sun was still not out and it was a cold day, they felt a vague joy.

Sitting by the window next to his wife, Mr. Parvin turned his head toward the street and gently removed his eye patch. He shut his good eye. The car moved fast; the images of the kaleidoscope whirled, turned, and changed shapes rapidly. Mr. Parvin saw the bricklayer approaching from the margins of the freeway. The old man motioned to him to stop. The bricklayer shouldn't enter the car. They couldn't talk now. But it was too late. Mr. Parvin's friend was already sitting on the front seat, managing to fit himself between Sharah and her mother. He turned back to look at Mr. Parvin.

"The surgery, huh?"

Mr. Parvin nodded.

"I just came to say, don't worry. I'll be around."

Mr. Parvin smiled, pulling the eye patch back up over his eye.

This was the first happy meal they had had in a long time. The whole family sat around Mr. Parvin's bed in the small hospital room. Sharah sat at her grandfather's feet. Mr. Parvin leaned against the pillows with a thick bandage around his head. Everybody was taking bites from their fat sandwiches, the thick mayonnaise dripping on their hands and wrists. The twins talked at the same time with full mouths. Bibi was reporting the possibility of a new job in an Italian restaurant. The owner had told her that she looked Italian and that she could pretend to be from Italy. The son-in-law was saying that the house was almost ready. Mr. and Mrs. Parvin could move in within a week.

Mr. Parvin didn't eat most of his sandwich. When they asked him why he wasn't eating, he said he was keeping a few bites for Gorgi. The girls looked at each other and burst into tears. Sharah cried, too, spilling her soda on the hospital blanket. The family ate the rest of their food in silence. When they all left, Mr. Parvin looked at the window and saw the clear blue sky and the top of a white tower. He touched his bandage. He was tempted to remove it, but he didn't. He feared blood and pain. He closed his open eye and tried to see the image of the bricklayer in the darkness of his head. He saw him for a second, but then the image blurred and disappeared. This was seeing him with his mind's eye. Mr. Parvin wanted the real man.

That sleepless night Mr. Parvin spent most of his time watching the head of the white tower swimming in the darkening sky. He wondered who lived there.

When they removed Mr. Parvin's bandages, Sharah screamed, "Grandpa has two eyes!" Everybody laughed.

Leaving the hospital, Mr. Parvin took a final glance at the white tower. He wanted to know what that place was, but he didn't ask. Now both of his eyes were open. He had to wear a dark patch to protect the sensitive eye. No kaleidoscope, no diamonds and circles. In the car, he looked silently at the fast-passing views. His son-in-law took them all to see the new house.

"This is beautiful!" the girls laughed, running through the empty house. Sharah was overjoyed and hollered and screamed. Her voice echoed in the empty rooms. Mr. Parvin's son-in-law walked him from one room to another, showing him the house. A very old house with fresh paint. A better neighborhood than theirs. A yard, an oak tree, green grass, and a bench facing two identical crepe myrtles, now dry, but promising to bloom early in the spring. Mrs. Parvin opened all the kitchen cabinets; she pulled all the drawers out.

The Parvins moved a few days later. They had few possessions to bring with them. They took some of Abi's furniture and planned to buy more in the future. Bibi moved in with them and started her restaurant job. Mrs. Parvin and her son-in-law took Mr. Parvin to another doctor, a psychiatrist. He wrote a prescription for Mr. Parvin's depression and occasional hallucinations. Then his son-in-law took him to a barber shop to cut his long hair. Having so many chores in their new house, Mrs. Parvin no longer had time to wash and comb her husband's hair.

On the barber's raised chair, Mr. Parvin sat staring at himself with both eyes open. The barber talked and clipped his silky hair. Feeling the old man's bump under his fingers, the barber asked what that little walnut was. Mr. Parvin's son-in-law explained that when his father-in-law was a boy, he fell out of a tree, and that's how the bump grew there. Mr. Parvin either didn't understand the conversation or paid no attention to it. He was immersed in a scene he was watching in the barber's mirror. Through the open door of the shop he saw a half-built structure across the street. A worker stood on a scaffold laying bricks on top of bricks. Mr. Parvin watched him and waited patiently until the barber was done. When they left the shop, he turned toward the building, raised his head, and looked up. The worker turned to see him. The intense sun shone directly in the worker's eyes. He held his broad hand over his brow and gazed at Mr. Parvin for a long second. As if finally recognizing the old man, he smiled. The creases of his sun-burnt forehead were smoothed away, and his white teeth gleamed in the light. Mr. Parvin smiled back and winked at the worker, feeling a tickling joy he hadn't felt in a long time. Knowing now that the bricklayer would always be around, he let his son-in-law take him home.

Death Observed

Khanum-jun decided to die a week before my birthday. It didn't change much, though. I just had my party a week later. All I remember of *Khanum-jun* is her silver braided hair and the sight of two white pills on her warm, red tongue even after they tried to force them down with two glasses of water. Everyone was sad, especially my grandfather, *Khanum-jun's* son. I didn't know what to tell him. He was an only child like me. He visited *Khanum-jun* every single Monday. I knew that I had to be sad too but it wasn't any worse than when I'd leave your house at two in the morning not knowing if I would ever see you again. It was toward the end of whatever we had made out of what was between us, and when it ended, something bigger than my great-grandmother died. You knew I was an only child. I had shown you photos—black-and-white ones from when I was five. But it ended anyway. Something kept pounding at me after that. Something that still follows me at two in the morning as I drive down the freeway. It makes me smoke although I've quit. That pounding. It never goes away, even though I'm happy now.

Agha-jun died, too. My grandfather on my father's side of the family. Cancer ate at him until there was nothing left. Everyone wore black and mourned. We sat around a big throw and ate halva. He was thin and tall and had never looked at me. He never bought me anything for *Eid* either. Once again I knew that I had to be sad but it wasn't worse than when my uncle left for Turkey to finish his studies. I gave him a color photo of him and me standing in snow up to our knees and a letter. In the photo he has my striped scarf around his head like a turban and has a broad smile on his face. I have my bright yellow plastic boots on and my hair is in pigtails. I knew my mother would be upset if she discovered that I took that photo out of my album. She found out later on and did get upset. But my uncle left anyway. On a big bus. Nothing held him back. And then you left, and everyone else left until I was alone. All alone. Everyone left. At least if they died I would be sure that they're gone. But they're out there somewhere getting by without me. Meanwhile, memories haunt me, and that thing still pounds away. It pounds away even though I'm happy now.

NAHID RACHLIN

Search

As I pack my bags, my eyes continually find their way to the photo-graph of my mother and me that sits on my desk. Finally, my sister, Lily, and I are ready for our trip to Iran to find Mother. We will leave in three days and be there in four, losing one day to travel. It took six months to get the visas. We had to prove the existence of our mother and relatives in Iran and had to get new passports with photos taken in proper Islamic attire—hair covered by scarves and bodies hidden in raincoats. We will have to dress this way when we get there and follow the strict codes laid out by the new regime. Even purchasing airline tickets was difficult since few airlines fly to Iran these days. Of course, it will all be worth the effort if we finally track her down.

In the photograph, both Mother and I are dressed up. I am wear-ing a blue dress with a pleated skirt, a blue ribbon in my hair, white shoes, and socks. She is wearing a chocolate-colored dress, high heels, and a hat. Black hair flows over her shoulders. She is slender. Her eyes are dark and dreamy, her lips almost heart-shaped. I must have been ten or eleven at the time the photograph was taken—a few years before she left us. Could the photo have been taken the day I looked up at her as we stood on the steps of the church, and I saw tears rolling down her face? Later that day, I found her sitting in a chair by the window in her room smoking a cigarette, looking sad and withdrawn. "What's wrong, Mother?" I asked. "I miss my sisters, my family," she said in her heavily accented English, adding, "This isn't the way I was raised." Only later did I understand what she meant: she had converted to Catholicism to please my father and his family.

Fourteen years ago she had vanished from our lives—I was only thirteen and Lily was eleven, but the wound is still fresh. How could she have vanished like that? At first she sent presents with short notes for me, Lily, and later for my son, Darien. But she never gave a return address. I still have some of the gifts—a pink-and-blue hand-knit sweater (which no longer fits me), a flower-shaped barrette (that I still wear sometimes even though it is old), and a doll with black braids that I keep on my dresser. I used to take it to bed with me. As I held the doll, thinking about my mother, a warm and comforting wave of feelings would envelope me. I would see my mother's face close to mine, feel her arm around me, hear her whispering to me, telling me stories, the way she used to before she left. After a while, the notes and gifts stopped coming. I wrote her many letters, sending them to Aunt Mahin to forward to her, begging her to come back, asking forgiveness for the mischievous things Lily and I had done, which were, I was certain, one of the reasons she had gone away. I promised to be a good girl, to obey her. I wrote about lonely nights and how empty the house was without her. Then I wrote to Aunt Mahin, asking why Mother did not answer my letters, but she never gave me any answers. I had horrible visions of Mother being locked up in a mental hospital or worse, dead.

Then a letter arrived six months ago and ignited the idea for a trip to Iran. I noticed the air-mailed letter among the envelopes I pulled out of the mailbox one day when I came home from work. Was it from my mother? My heart almost leapt out of my chest at the mere thought. I dashed inside, dropped my bag on the living room floor, and opened the letter. I know more Persian now than when Mother lived with us—learning it has been part of my obsession with her. The letter was from Aunt Mahin:

I passed your letter and the photograph on to your mother. She said she's glad that you have your father's house to return to. And Darien is such a lovely child. She cried when she saw his picture. All I can tell you about your mother is not to worry. She is fine, and she thinks about you, Lily, and your father all the time. She has never stopped loving you. But keeping a distance is the only way she can live her new life, one that suits her better. . . .

I breathed deeply, painfully. Perhaps the decisive force behind her finally responding after all these years, even though it was no more than a brief message sent through her sister, was the letter I wrote to her:

I'm back living with Dad. Divorced. Darien is four years old. I wish I had you to talk to in the midst of all this. Lily, too, just broke up with someone she was going out with. A lot of broken hearts here . . . How are you, are you happy?

I had enclosed a new picture of Darien with the letter. Did Mother see my moving in with my father as a desperate act, stirring guilt in her for not being here for me? Was she feeling guilty or did it simply make her yearn for what she had left behind? Was it strange that I have moved in with my father at the age of twenty-seven, with a four-year-old son? A weakness? There are, of course, many benefits. I can save on rent and go back to school with the money from the sale of the house Chuck and I had lived in. And Darien has more space to run around at Dad's. His new room once belonged to Lily and is almost as large as the entire apartment we had moved into right after the divorce. Anyway, I love the house, with its views of the beach from practically every room and its huge palm-filled yard.

I close the suitcase and go into the kitchen to get dinner ready. As I beat the eggs for a cake, I think of coloring eggs with Lily for Easter when we were kids. Mother would add designs to them: stripes, dots, little chickens. We would pile up the eggs in a basket and put it on the dining room table. I vividly remember the last time I saw Mother. She was wearing a blue linen dress and navy low-heeled shoes. I can't recall whether she was carrying any luggage or whether, before walking out the door forever, she had displayed any extra affection toward Lily and me.

Dad had tried to be both father and mother to us. He came directly home from work to shop and cook. He read or told us stories at night. Most of the time, he put up a cheerful front, but once I caught him crying; he was leaning on the patio railing in the twilight, holding his head between his hands, and tears were streaming down his face. I asked him what was wrong, and he held me against his body, saying, "Nothing, nothing, life just gets sad sometimes." I couldn't help myself. "Daddy you won't go away from us like Mommy did, will you?" "No, no, of course not," he said, wiping his tears and pulling me up into his arms. "I'll be here with you forever." But insecurity lingered with me. I asked him over and over, "Do you love me?" He was always reassuring. "You and Lily are my whole life; I love you more than you can imagine." He gave us as much as any father could, but all his attention didn't compensate for the loss and the trauma of Mother's sudden departure.

Dad comes in and helps me set the table. The dining room is filled with light because of its south-facing windows. We eat on the same thick oak table we sat at as children. Underneath it are carvings Lily and I made: a round, smiling face and a tree. I used to do my homework at this table while I watched Mother work in the kitchen. My interest in school and studying declined after she left. It all seemed so irrelevant. In the classroom, I would daydream about my mother instead of listening to the teachers. I would imagine us in a room with no one and no sounds to disrupt our complete focus on each other. Indifference to school followed me all the way to college. When I dropped out after one semester, one of my teachers said, "You aren't living up to your potential."

Dad and I sit down to eat with Darien on a chair between us. Dad attends to Darien, cutting up a piece of veal for him and wiping the sauce off his face. Dad is much more subdued than I remember. He used to be loud and assertive. He liked to joke around and would spontaneously turn on music and start dancing with Mother or with Lily or me.

Darien gets up from the table and turns on the television. He

179

changes channels until he finds cartoons and takes his plate off the table to eat by the television.

I ask Dad, "How was your day at work?"

"Not so good. One of the young women got hysterical and threatened suicide."

"No! Anyone I met when I came there?"

"Janis, the red-headed, freckled girl."

"I remember her."

Suddenly, Dad says, "The happiest days for your mother were just after each of you was born. She's going to come back. She'll want to claim her family one day," he adds more forcefully, as if he sees a clear analogy. "I work with runaways, I know they eventually want to return home." Maybe in the back of his mind he still thinks of my mother as young, like when he first met her. "You and Lily could try to bring her back."

He and Mother never officially divorced. Once, when I asked him why he said, "You know how hard it is for a Catholic to get divorced" (though he is no longer a practicing Catholic). And then, "Anyway she's going to come back."

They had met in Iran when he had gone there to represent a pharmaceutical company (he later quit that job and began studying to become a social worker). He had met her at a friend's house. Within a few months they were engaged, though they hardly knew each other. She had pleaded with her parents to let her marry him. At first, they opposed the marriage because he was American, but they reluctantly gave in later. She was eighteen and my father was twenty-five when they married. After they moved to the United States, Mom started college, but she quit and decided to stay home when Lily and I were born. Mother had developed an interest in painting flowers (a few of her paintings—a bunch of tulips, a large iris, two roses—hang on the walls of the living room). These are the bare facts. The rest—the yearning, the pain, the blame, and self-blame following her departure—are more elusive. Lily, Dad, and I have gone over the events so many times that they have come to re-semble rounded, washed stones, the kind you find at the bottom of a stream.

After dinner, Dad helps me clean up, then goes to his room, and I take Darien into the bathroom to give him his nightly bath. It is seven o'clock. Andy is half an hour late. I almost wish I had not started see-ing him again when he came back to L.A. from New York. He stays up all night watching old movies and works a few hours a day as a paralegal, barely making a living and writing scripts, with the hope that he will have a breakthrough someday. His hair is always di-sheveled and almost as long as mine. He is the opposite of Chuck, my ex-husband. Life had run smoothly for a while with Chuck, mostly because of his commitment and dedication. As the manager of a su-permarket, he had devised an elaborate filing system for the bills, for every bit of money that came and went, and for receipts to be used in preparing tax returns. He was good at fixing things around the house. It was this resourcefulness and attention to detail that helped pro-mote him from clerk to the position of manager.

What exactly went wrong between us? I remember a vague de-pression settling in and growing with time. Even simple things be-fuddled me. Am I doing the right thing rushing to Darien every time he starts to cry? Do I give in to his demands for milk or give him the pacifier too quickly? I was filled with self-doubt. Is it wrong to put him in our bed when he wanders into our room at dawn? "You've be-come impossible," Chuck said, when he came home and found me sit-ting idly on the sofa with the house in a jumbled mess. Sometimes he stormed out of the house and didn't come back until the middle of the night. Then one evening he said, "I can't take this any more," and left me for good.

The phone rings, and I pick it up.

"Hi, I'm going to be an hour late." It is Andy. "I'm working on an important point in the script."

"You're already half an hour late."

"I know. You understand, don't you?"

"I guess so." I should find someone new, instead of hanging on to this problematic relationship.

I end up meeting Andy at the eight o'clock showing of *Sleepless in Seattle*, a movie we hadn't planned on seeing. As we watch, he keeps whispering in my ear how he would do certain lines and scenes in the movie differently. After the film is over we go to Rioja, a Mexican restaurant that has just opened. We sit in a dim corner in the back, drink sangria, and order combination plates while we continue talking about the movie. It is more than I can bear.

We go to his apartment in a run-down section of Venice and head directly to the bedroom. I wonder if sex is what keeps us together. We are good together in bed. He likes making love in different spots of his apartment but mostly right here, where two large mirrors on the walls reflect our bodies as they intertwine and lock inside of each other.

When we lie back, sweaty and spent, all I feel is emptiness.

"What are you thinking about?" he asks.

"Nothing."

"You can't be thinking about nothing."

"Don't you ever wonder where we're heading?"

"No."

We get out of bed and go into his small living room.

"I'll get you some herb tea," he says and goes into the tiny kitchen while I sit on the sofa. Foam shows through torn spots in the fabric. He comes back with peppermint tea for me in the red polka dot cup he knows I like and a beer for himself. He sits next to me.

"So you feel good about going to Iran?" he asks.

"Happy and nervous. You know, I still miss my mother."

"Yeah. I can understand, sweetie. I missed my father for years, still do, after he and my mom split and he went to live in Mexico."

The television, which Andy never turns off, drones in the background. He intermittently drifts away from our conversation and focuses on the images on the screen. His own screenplays echo what he watches: sitcoms, mysteries, soap operas. His connection with what goes on around him is somewhat tenuous, but maybe mine is too.

I leave before midnight. At home, I tiptoe into Darien's room and check on him. He is asleep, so I go to my own room and get ready for bed. I have a hard time sleeping; I toss and turn. It's good that living here keeps me from spending too much time with Andy. I would never stay in his apartment an entire night or let him spend a night here, where Darien and Dad would overhear conversations and the creaking of the bed. Dad is reticent about the women in his life. In fact, he has never specifically mentioned or introduced anyone to me. He has acknowledged only having "women friends." Every year I expect him to announce to us that a romance has developed in his life, someone just widowed or divorced, or a woman he met at work, but nothing like that has happened yet.

I finally fall asleep and later wake from a dream about Mother. The two of us are standing together at the rail of a cruise ship. We are wearing identical red dresses, black patent-leather shoes, and gold necklaces. Mother begins to laugh. "They're going to get us mixed up," she says.

The dream seemed so real. I do resemble Mother. Lily has always looked more like Dad; she has his light brown hair and blue-gray eyes. I used to think I was closer to Mother than Lily was, that being the first-born brought me closer to her, and that Lily was closer to Dad. Now Lily rarely visits our father; she keeps herself busy, maybe too busy, with her job in Bullock's cosmetics department and with a string of boyfriends.

In two days we'll be in Isfahan . . . we'll be with Mother. Images of the one time she took Lily and me, as children, to Iran for a visit return to me in bright flashes. We stayed in a big house in a village just outside of Isfahan, an oasis on the edge of a beautiful desert. There were mountains in the distance, and they changed color from brown in the sun to salmon at dusk and then turned a deep blue with the darkening sky. Next to the house was an orchard with a spring in the middle of it. Lily and I and other local children roamed through the orchard, picked and ate fruit from the trees, and swam in the spring. At night, we slept under mosquito nets in the courtyard, where the stars and the moon were brighter than I had ever seen. I remember the sounds of that visit—the whistles of nightingales at dawn, the howl of the owls in the evening, and the shriek of the jackals in the middle of the night, which made me crawl into Mother's bed for protection. And the voice of the muezzin three times a day calling people to prayer. Many, many relatives came to the big house and fussed over Lily and me. They gave us presents—jewelry, clay animals, rag dolls. I remember Mother whispering things to her relatives about religion, a certain concern on their faces at what she said, a certain nervousness on her part. These images and sounds have come back to me repeatedly over the years, like a dream; they are so disconnected from our lives in L.A.

Except for that visit, Mother kept a distance from her own culture. She followed another religion, observed different holidays from the ones she grew up with, spoke English instead of her native Persian. We, her children, were all-American, and she had done little to help us understand or be a part of her culture. But, in general, she wasn't really a part of American culture. She kept to herself, had few friends. She was shy with other mothers. She never went to open house at our school or to PTA meetings. At our birthday parties, it was Dad who took charge, decorating the house with balloons and colorful streamers, arranging games, and preparing party favors for the children to take home. She smiled pleasantly at the other mothers but rarely engaged them in conversation. When she left us, Dad lied. "She's sick, she went to recuperate at her family's house." But as time went by and there was no sign of her, he said, "Don't worry, one day you'll come home and see her waiting for you."

We have been in Isfahan for five days and have only five more days before we return. Lily and I must go back to work, and I can't bear the separation from Darien. I keep wondering what he is doing, though I know that between Dad and his baby-sitter, he's fine.

The long flight to Tehran from L.A. via Turkey and then the bus ride from Tehran to Isfahan passed quickly. Lily and I were so intensely engaged in our speculations about Mother. The hotel, in the center of the city near the main square, is modern and filled with foreign businessmen. When we arrived, we immediately freshened up, had a snack in the dining room, and set out on our search for Mother. But when we arrived at Aunt Mahin's house we were told by a young girl who answered the door that she had moved away. This was strange since Aunt Mahin's address had always been the same. "Are you sure?" I asked. The girl stared at me, looking insulted. She said she didn't know my aunt's new address.

Now I continue my search alone, without Lily's help. After our first frenzied attempt, Lily has been taking tours arranged through the hotel while I have been trying to trace Mother through shopkeepers, the bank, and the post office. I have done little else. I allowed myself to visit only a few sights in this ancient city: the Shaking Minarets, a building that sways when you lean against it, and the Masjid-e-Shah, a mosque with beautiful Islamic architecture.

I notice a photography shop among a row of stores displaying handmade vases, painted pen cases, and silver jewelry. I look at the photographs behind the window—one of a family together, one of a bride and groom. I go inside and ask the woman standing behind the counter, "Do you have any photographs of the Anjomani family? I'm a relative from America."

"Yes, some we took at a wedding. There have been several weddings in the family."

Though I was hoping for it, I didn't expect her answer.

"Can I look at the photographs?"

She opens an album and quickly looks through it. Then she pauses on one page. A woman standing next to a man in a courtyard strongly resembles my mother. She is older, of course, but with the same features. The eyes are unmistakably hers.

"Is this Pari Anjomani?"

The woman nods. "And that is her husband."

Husband? My mother is still married to my father. The woman could be mistaking a relative for a husband. The man in the photograph is burly with coarse features and a big mustache twisted upward.

"Do you have her address?"

She fumbles through a stack of papers, mostly bills, and receipts on the desk. "Here is Pari's address. They live in Ashtarjan."

"How far is that?"

"About an hour by bus." She writes down the address and gives it to me. She tells me how to find it among a maze of lanes. "Do you want me to take a photograph of you?" she asks. "As you can see, we do very good work."

"Definitely, I'll come back with my sister." I thank her and leave, eager to tell Lily what I have discovered.

Lily comes out of the bathroom with a towel wrapped around her, water glistening on her skin and dripping down her hair. I notice the large bruise on her arm, which she told me is from Jarred's playful bites. Her relationships with men worry me sometimes, although I am not proud of my own broken marriage and all the meaningless affairs I have had since.

When I tell her about the address I have found she says, "I hope it isn't a false lead."

Outside the window I see mist has gathered in the air, obscuring the view. Only the dome and minarets of a mosque are clearly visible. A brown finch comes and sits on the window sill, its wings wet, probably from bathing in the fountain in the hotel's courtyard.

Lily finishes drying herself and begins to dress. "I met a really cute French guy on the tour. He's gorgeous." She studies my face for my reaction. "I gave him the phone number here."

"Oh, Lily," I say in a tone I try to keep light.

After Lily gets dressed we go to eat in a restaurant near the hotel that serves the usual *chelo kebab* and *khoreshes*.

A waiter comes over to take our order. Lily smiles at him. He smiles back flirtatiously, lingers a bit, trying to talk to her in English. She looks striking even though her hair is all covered up.

After the waiter walks away she says, "I wonder what happened to Maurice."

"Who's Maurice?"

"You know, the man I met on the tour. He didn't call."

"You know you're playing with fire. This is an Islamic country. We're covered up because we aren't supposed to be temptations to men. You can get arrested and go to jail if you're seen with a man who isn't your husband, brother, or father."

"Don't worry, I'll be careful . . . if I ever see him again."

After we finish eating we walk for a while through the main square, which is bright with gas lamps. Many people, the women wearing chadors or *rupushes* and scarves, are walking around, going in and out of shops, or sitting in restaurants and cafés.

When we return to the hotel, the clerk hands Lily a message.

"He did call," she says to me, showing me the pink slip.

I glance at the message: "Maurice requested that you call him back." Underneath the message is the phone number.

"Are you going to call him?"

"Maybe."

Trying to talk her out of it would have had little effect.

Later as we lie in bed I feel like we are children again, close and yet separated by our different dreams. But what are my dreams exactly? Sometimes it's as if I were a character I am reading about in a bad novel.

I wake in the morning with the rays of the sun on my face. Lily is not in her bed. I look at my watch. It's ten o'clock. I have overslept. I get up and start for the bathroom. I see my name written in large letters on a yellow sheet of paper lying on the night table, and I pick it up. A note from Lily.

"Miriam, I hope you don't mind, but I'm going to spend the day with Maurice. I found him waiting for me in the lobby this morning. You go on your search alone, see you tonight."

I cringe inwardly. How could she spend this, of all days, with a man she will never see again once we leave Iran? Is she more pessimistic than I am or more indifferent to Mother? I think of her as a teenager telling her friends that Mother had died. Right after Mother left us, though, we talked about it all the time. Sometimes I would wake in the middle of the night and hear Lily crying in her room.

I get off the bus in Ashtarjan and walk along the river that runs through it, passing a mosque, houses built of mud or stone huddled together on the other side, green pastures, and a few orchards. I have covered up even more carefully, wearing my darkest scarf and a plain gray *rupush*, which I bought to replace my raincoat. The sunlight, so lucid and golden, adds luster to everything, and the most squalid sights take on richness. The snow-covered mountains surrounding the village seem like a shelter against harsh desert winds. It is cool as I walk.

I come to a little square with shops that carry the essentials: sugar, rice, matches. A mill, a low clay building with a tower, stands on one side of the square and a dilapidated boarding house is on the other end. Then I come to a cluster of narrow lanes snaking off a main, wide avenue and begin to look for the address. At an intersection stands a mosque with a group of women wearing black chadors sitting on its steps, waiting for something. Next to the mosque is a huge poplar tree with a hollow in its center. An old man is lying on a mat spread in the hollow. Children have gathered around him; they taunt him and throw coins to him. I keep thinking what a different world this is from L.A. and wonder how my mother, who had lived in L.A. for so many years, could live here.

I see Gol Abad—the name of the village—written on the wall of an alley. There it is, I think excitedly and turn onto it. One side of the alley is lined with gardens and orchards filled with flowers and fruit trees that peer above the crude walls. There are houses on the other side. Some of the houses' doors are open, and I have glimpses of hall-ways, courtyards. In one hallway two children are kneeling and playing with marbles. I arrive in front of number 28. I stand back and look at it. It is an old, sagging house with weathered blue tiles that surround the dark, heavy door. The house's appearance is soft-ened a little by the row of small fruit trees in front of it and by the golden sunlight. The mere thought that my mother might be inside there fills me with awe and excitement. I hear my own heart beat as I ring the rusty bell. It has been fourteen years since I saw her last—how will she react to my showing up at her house unannounced? How will she explain leaving us? My heart flutters almost as if I am about to reunite with a lover. I put my head on the door and listen for sounds inside. I hear children's voices and then a woman's barely au-dible voice. I begin to cough. I remember when Mother left us, I de-veloped a cough that would not go away. Father took me to a doctor who gave me a prescription. Later, when I was older, he told me the medicine was a placebo; the doctor had said my cough was due to nervousness.

"Mother, someone is knocking," I hear a boy saying. Footsteps follow. Could I have the wrong address, the wrong person?

The door opens and a small boy stands before me, staring at me with his dark eyes.

"I'm looking for Pari Anjomani. Does she live here?"

The boy runs back inside. "Mother, Mother," he yells.

I stand frozen in my spot. A moment later I see a woman approaching in the dim hallway. My eyes are glued to her, and as she comes closer I can see that she is the same woman in the photograph who strongly resembles Mother. "Are you Pari?" I ask through my tightened throat.

She nods, staring at me without recognition.

This may be a different Pari altogether. But her eyes . . . "Do you know who I am?" I ask. "Miriam." She keeps staring.

She waves her hand in the air as if about to shut the door on me. Then she says, "Oh, Miriam, Miriam, you came, why did you . . . I'm so happy to see you . . . you shouldn't have come," she says in a confused whisper.

"Mother, I've been searching for you, Lily and I."

I walk into the hallway, and we embrace tightly.

"Please don't tell my other children who you are. I'll explain everything, my Miriam, my dear daughter."

My mother's four children, two boys and two girls, ranging in age from around four to ten, play in the courtyard while she and I sit in the living room talking. Chickens and goats are roaming around the courtyard. I recall how frequently I would come home, in L.A., and find Mother leaning over a flower bed, weeding, planting, watering. And then those flower paintings. I don't see any paintings like them on her walls here, but the courtyard before us is flush with flowers.

The walls are whitewashed, the floors covered with tiles, chipped here and there, the furniture is simple and hard. On the worn mosaic-covered mantle above the stone fireplace are a few enlarged, framed photographs and clay animals.

"Let me get you something to eat," she says.

"I'm not hungry."

"Why didn't Lily come with you?"

I hesitate and grope for an answer. "She had to rest. She had a stomachache."

"Why don't I get you a cool drink. *Doogh, sharbat?*"

"*Doogh* is fine." I detect a strange formality in my tone.

She gets up and so do I. We go into the kitchen. The kitchen is large, also with whitewashed walls, and it smells pleasantly of spices. Baskets heaped with fruit or with garlic, onions, and other vegetables lie on a tiled counter; copper pots and pans hang from hooks. She takes out a jug of *doogh* from a stumpy-looking ice box, pours some in two glasses, and we go back into the living room.

I am hoping she will say our letters never got to her, that she will explain her hiding from us, that she will say she never knew we had been trying so hard to get her back, but another voice in a deep gray spot of my mind asks, how can any of that be possible?

She says suddenly, "I'm sorry I haven't been in touch."

"Haven't been in touch" is too light a phrase to capture the magnitude of the loss I have been living with, but everything about this woman, my mother, is startling, verging on the absurd, unbelievable. I am not the same person I was when she left. I have been through a divorce; I have a child; I have moved out and back into my father's house. Some of my dreams have been shattered, substituted by others. Why do I expect Mother to be the same as years ago?

She begins to knit, with blue and green yarn. "A sweater for my youngest son," she says.

Memories, half-faded, spill over me. My mother, younger than she is now, sitting under a tree, knitting a sweater then, too, for Lily or me. She and Lily standing in the living room of our house, arguing about something. Lily saying to her with the bluntness and cruelty of a child, "Mother, you don't understand, you're from another culture." And me, ashamed of Mother's accent, blushing when she speaks to my friends. Mother crying and saying, "I don't know what's the matter with me."

"Mother, why have you been hiding from us? Tell me, what made you leave?"

My mother hangs her head down and does not say anything. When she lifts her head I see her eyes are glistening with tears. We both take sips of our yogurt drinks, and I have a momentary illusion of closeness to her, the way I did as a child, sitting with her, feeling protected. So many times I have woken up in the middle of the night from dreams about Mother, so often I have lain in the dark thinking of questions I would ask her if I ever came face-to-face with her. During those moments, I felt that some piece of my own existence would always be missing unless I saw her, talked to her.

Two hours later we're still sitting there, and I'm still urging her to talk to me, to tell me what happened. Finally she begins to talk:

"One day I was alone in the house. You and Lily were at school, and your father was out working. I was depressed. There was a knock on the door. I went to open it, thinking maybe it was a neighbor, though I had not really become friendly with any of them. When I opened the door I saw a man standing there. He said abruptly, in a familiar tone as if he knew me, 'I finally found you, do you know how long I've been looking?' I couldn't believe it, but it was Parviz, a boy I had known in our neighborhood. He had asked my parents to let him marry me, and I would have, if your father hadn't come along. I was so shaken to see him . . . 'It's just a friendly visit,' he told me."

But then they had gone for a walk in Marina Del Rey. They talked about old times. After a while Mother fell into a state, some kind of delirium. She was not sure where she was, in what country, beside what body of water. Was not sure about her age or who this man was, holding her arm. His presence, his touch, had both calmed and excited her. What calmed her was his mere presence, and what excited her was what his presence had opened up; he had punctured a capsule in which powerful memories had been bottled up. His visit pulled on her like a magnet in the days that followed. Suddenly everything around her—the beaches, the pastel colors, the precarious-looking houses, the canyons still holding rubble from fires, charred hillsides where houses had once stood—seemed desolate and meaningless.

She stops speaking. I am too dazed to say anything. I remember how she used to withdraw into some inner location, and now I see it as a retreat on her part. She could no longer bear what was going on around her. Still, her dreamy look, her long periods of sitting in a corner and staring into the darkness, had not seemed to signal anything so drastic. Finally I ask, "Is that the person you live with now?"

She nods. Then she startles me by saying, "We got married when I came here."

"But you're still married to my father," I answer.

"No one here knows that, except for Parviz, of course. It would have terrible consequences for me if they knew," she says in a pleading tone.

My eyes focus on the pictures on the mantle. I spot a man that looks like the one in the other photograph I saw in the shop. "Did you ever love Dad?" I ask.

"I was very young when we met. I was swept away by the idea of living in America. But it took every ounce of my will to try to adjust to it. I did my best, but something broke when I saw Parviz; it would have happened sooner or later anyway. There was a lack I couldn't fill."

I think of the lack I have been feeling for so long, which seems to have stunted my growth. I assume the same is true about Lily. We have been blown this way and that like unanchored ships tossed by the wind.

"True, he's possessive, jealous, but in some ways I feel more free with him than I ever did with your dad," my mother says. "We can laugh together."

One of her daughters comes over to us. My mother says to her, "She's a friend visiting from America." Then turning to me she says, "This is my oldest daughter, Manijeh."

I smile at Manijeh. She stares at me with large, dark eyes, leans over and whispers something to Mother who then whispers something back. Then Manijeh dashes out.

"She wanted to know if you're staying here. My children love having visitors. She wanted to bake something for you. She's a wonderful child, perfect."

She is a substitute for me, I think painfully.

Mother looks animated now; her eyes are glistening. And I become aware that the house, in spite of its decaying condition, is filled with happiness and warmth.

"What does he . . . ?" I have a hard time saying "your husband," and an equally hard time saying his name.

"He's a carpenter; he builds cabinets, closets," she answers assuringly. There is a touch of pride in her tone. "He's a good man." She reaches forward and holds my hand. I feel a tremor in her hand. "But Miriam, if you love me, if you truly care about my well-being and happiness, you have to promise to forget about me, at least for a while longer. I have no choice."

I nod and think of my father still hoping for her return, his saying to me, so many times, his face thoughtful, furrows between his brows, "I work with runaways, I know they eventually want to reclaim their families."

"I'd better go back," I say, looking at my watch. "There's only one bus going to Isfahan this afternoon. It leaves in half an hour."

"Wait," she says. She walks into the adjacent room and comes back out, holding something in her hand. "Here, I want you to have this, a memento." It is a gold necklace—a heart with a tiny latch on it, hanging from a gold chain.

"Open it," she says.

I open the heart, expecting a photograph of her, instead it's of her four children, a row of tiny heads.

"Remember me by them," she says.

I put the necklace in my purse and get up. We walk to the door together. We pause a moment and then embrace. As I pull away, I see her face from memory: warm, dreamy, but also discontented. When I return to the present, to her face as I see it now, it is peaceful and contented. Outside, before I turn around, I hear Manijeh's voice from the yard. "Did the American leave already?"

"Yes," my mother says without elaborating.

I walk at a brisk pace to the bus station. Moving calms me down a little. What is Lily going to think, what will her reaction be other than, "I always knew she had forgotten us"? Maybe I am better off keeping silent about my meeting with Mother. A secret, no one, not even Lily, has to know about. But I know I will have to tell her. Just before I reach the bus station, I take the heart Mother gave me from my purse and throw it into the river. I stand there for a moment and watch it sink and then gradually disappear. At that moment, I experience feeling of clarity. I am finally free of the heaviness and constraint. I can begin to focus on my own happiness. After all, that's what Mother has done.

Tuesdays

FOR M.

It's late November in Los Angeles, almost ten o'clock on a chilly Tuesday night. I turn right on Third Street toward La Brea. Babak's looking out the window, but he avoids looking at the blonde in the car next to us.

"Baab, how much've you got?" I ask.

"Enough," he murmurs.

"How much?" I ask again.

"About sixty bucks . . . enough!"

"I have thirty-five. Should be okay."

"Yeah, it is," he says indifferently.

I know he's excited about tonight although he doesn't show it.

"Let's eat. I'm hungry," I say to him.

"Sure. Where?" he asks, still looking out and still avoiding the blonde.

"Pink's?"

"Na . . . I don't want any fast food."

"It's not fast food anymore. They call it 'comfort food' now."

He turns and gives me an irreverent look.

Babak and I have known each other forever it seems. He is more of a brother to me than my own. Our first encounter was outside an elementary school in Tehran where he was a grade above me. Now, in our early thirties, half a world away from where we grew up, we meet once a week on Tuesdays.

In Los Angeles—the so-called largest refuge of Iranians outside the old country—Babak is probably my last hope for a family, and I suspect I have become his, too. Suffering from the perpetual fear of being too Iranian, and caught in the oblivion of not belonging among our own kind and never being accepted by the people whose country we live in, Babak and I are each other's occasional and sole source of comfort.

On Tuesday nights we meet after dark, eat somewhere unplanned, cruise around Los Angeles until eleven, and then spend the night deep in the belly of an old building—a nightclub that plays healing music: a blend of industrial and gothic, the kind of music I would call pure anguish.

Tuesday is different from other days. It's beyond the banality of weekends. There's a mood of excitement and a sense of anticipation; it often generates an anxiety similar to what I felt as a kid while waiting outside an airport terminal, whether departing myself or waiting for someone to arrive. It seems that time on Tuesdays is pregnant with possibilities and obscures the knowledge that many of those possibilities will eventually dissolve into disappointments or washed-up illusions. It's a good night to be alive.

To make things easier for himself, Babak has arranged to be off on Wednesdays. He doesn't want the terror of the next day's work to ruin Tuesday night. I, however, still have to get up at six and turning in at three in the morning makes it difficult. But, I wouldn't change Tuesdays or give them up, not even for sleep.

"So? Where are we eating?" I ask, keeping my eyes on the road.

"I know . . . let's go to RED, I like their food," he answers as he reaches for one of my cigarettes.

"Are you nuts?" I protest.

"Why?"

"Have you looked at yourself?!" I glance at his pants. He looks down and frowns.

"What is it? You're not saying you're better dressed than I am?" he asks, irritated.

"No! Just more versatile," I reply.

This is a sore subject between us. Babak's outfits on Tuesdays usually consist of military gear in different shades of camouflage with weird accessories. I suspect no one can distinguish him from a soldier gone AWOL. I lost my devotion to army overcoats and my fetish for American military paraphernalia once I left Iran, but Babak still dresses like the old goons back in high school. This is his armor for dancing to industrial music.

I put on a straight face and use a diplomatic tone.

"Look, you're wearing paratrooper's pants and a bomber jacket. Your hair is cut like a rooster's and your suspenders have bullet holders on them. You look like you've just dropped out of the sky and are ready for an invasion. I can go in there without distracting anyone, but you, looking like a soldier of fortune, you'll have all eyes on you. Baab, we can't go into a nice restaurant looking like militia men, you know that."

"You're such a . . . whatever . . . where then?" he asks giving up any response to my commentary.

"We'll go to that chicken place on Melrose you took me to once," I answer, relieved.

"Fine. Let's go."

I make a turn on Melrose and drive for a while before I reach the place. It's packed inside. There aren't any parking spots. I circle the block twice before I find a parking spot on the street.

Inside the restaurant, we do attract attention. Babak's paratrooper gear is a little too much, even for this place.

"What the fuck are these people looking at?" he asks, fuming.

"Your beautiful smile!" I answer sarcastically as I walk toward the cashier.

We sit down and order.

"Baab, you know what we need?" I ask with a straw between my teeth.

"What? A life?" he answers with a playful smile forming on his face.

"Funny!"

"Go ahead, tell me, what?"

"We need a female presence on Tuesdays."

"And what do you mean by a female presence?"

"A woman. You know what *female* means, don't you?"

"Sounds good, but why do we need her?"

"Sometimes a woman can put things into a different perspective, you know, make a comment or a gesture that puts a whole different spin on things. Believe me, I know. For one thing, she'll probably cure you of your paratrooper complex."

"Dream on. It's not a complex, it's a state of mind, a way of approaching the world."

"Whatever! The point is we could still use a female friend to soften this macho air."

"Fine, we'll find a female presence tonight. It will be interesting. We'll approach some woman and say: 'Excuse us, but we are auditioning for your kind of presence, would you like to try out for the part?' Who knows, maybe even the Iranian goth queen, what's her name . . . Roya . . . maybe even her," he says giggling.

"Don't laugh, somewhere in there you know I'm right," I snap at him.

Our food arrives. We both fall silent and start to eat. There are a couple of cops sitting two tables away from us. One of them, a female officer, eyes Babak, but she can tell he is harmless—even in military gear. She smiles at me, and I notice I am staring at her.

If it weren't for the lifetime of preparation we've had, we probably wouldn't be able to stand one another. Babak is private and desolate, a recluse who constantly digs deep within himself for answers that

are so much easier to find outside. A few external pleasures and comforts keep him content. He's programmed himself to believe beauty,
comfort, or luxury are meaningless. In an act of mental self-mutila-
tion, he's shut himself off to all that can be conventionally pleasing,
even the blonde woman in the car next to him. For him, nights like
these are about cleansing the system and enjoying the therapeutic
effects of going out, dancing, and listening to music. Whenever he's
even slightly infatuated by something material or organic, he calls it
"a bug in the program."

Ever since Babak left Iran and arrived here, he's been on a quiet cru-
sade against everyone and everything, chief among them himself. As-
suming the role of his therapist, I have continually failed to discern
the source of his malaise or to convince him to change. The more time
I spend with him and the deeper I dig, the less obvious the source of
his pain. He reminds me of something Camus once wrote: "[A]ll re-
bellions are nostalgia for innocence." I suspect he's still trying to res-
urrect an innocence he thinks he lost the day he walked off the plane
that landed him in this country.

I'm his opposite in many ways, but we're not too far off on the de-
viance spectrum. Like Babak, I'm a recluse and a hermit. But for me,
this world has one axis, one end: finding a sense of beauty and rel-
ishing in the promise of happiness that it provides, however false or
illusionary it may be. Sometimes—most of the time—it's a woman's
beautiful face or the cigarette that I smoke while driving on the freeway, or even the bitter taste of alcohol when that favorite track of
mine is being played on Tuesday nights, right about one in the morning, as I sink into the corner wall.

I'm not sure which one us has it worse, but I know both Babak and
I have a tremendous sense of unfulfilled longing that has mutated into
fragmented obsessions, strange behaviors, and distorted tastes—a
collection of emotional scars that we can share only with each other.
In the meantime, we both have our mental narcotics: a paranoia about

our own kind, a suspicion about what is distinctly American, and a profound separation from what is often comfortably normal. Through this apprehensive state of being, Babak suppresses his greatest wants into mere whispers, and my most minute desires become raging fires.

"Do you think she's gonna be there tonight?" he asks, breaking the silence.

"Who?" I ask, knowing who he is talking about, but pretending that I don't. "Roya?"

Roya is an Iranian woman, not much younger than we, who shows up religiously every Tuesday night at the nightclub. Armed with an incredibly beautiful face and dressed in black every time, she is one of the comforts of Tuesday night. She moves around in a body that seems as fragile as the thin stem of a wine glass. Dressed in her long black sleeveless dress, she appears out of nowhere, moves across the dance floor, and swirls gracefully to the music.

The second time I saw her, I asked the bouncer to look up her name for me. Out of fear that she might hear us talking about her, Babak and I have taken to calling her "Napalm." I named her that for her lava-colored hair and for the fact that her face makes one think of nothing else but how it can devastate. It's the sort of face that men leave or-dinary-looking women for and die in search of.

"I'm sure she's gonna be there," Babak says confidently.

"I'm gonna see if I can break the silence tonight. You know . . . kind of introduce myself."

"Really?" He acts surprised, but I know he's grown tired of my crushes.

"Yes. I have to get to know 'the gothic goddess.'"

"You'll go up to her and talk to her?"

"Uh-uh."

"We'll see. Good luck, and do it before the alcohol takes over!"

We leave the restaurant and get into the car. I grab a cigarette and offer one to Babak, and we both light up. I put the Crown Victoria into drive and turn on the music. Loud, shrieking voices fill the inside of the car.

Babak starts mimicking the music, and I drive east on Franklin. After few moments, I turn down the music.

"Baab."

"What?"

"What's gonna happen once this ends?"

"What ends?"

"This whole deal, Tuesday nights, the music, the people. I don't know . . . this whole deal, this whole period of our lives."

"Why does it have to end?"

"Because I'm thirty, you're thirty-one, and we are not acting or living like thirty-year-old Iranians."

"OK . . . how should thirty-year-olds act?"

"Normal. You know, sitting next to their wives on their weird-looking furniture, watching bleached blondes do shit-talk on Persian television, avoiding cholesterol, and setting up retirement accounts. You know, regular, normal stuff. And, look at us!"

He watches me from the corner of his eyes, then turns to face me.

"What about us?" he asks.

"You tell me."

It seems he's been waiting for that answer.

"Well, instead of a stupid sitcom or a Persian bitch screaming on TV, you're gonna feast on hammer noise set to music. Instead of listening to your wife nagging you about how she despises another woman for having just bought a white grand piano, you're gonna binge through a whole pack of Red and Whites, and instead of sleeping without even saying good-night to the woman next to you, you'll eye the woman at the other side of the room who looks like heaven outfitted in black wrapping paper. How's that? All this place lacks is the retirement package, and frankly, I don't think we're gonna live that long!"

"Heaven in black wrapping paper, huh?" I like his analogy. He knows how to push my buttons.

"Yes, and if you think this is no good, you can always leave it."

"What? Leave you with all this delicious anxiety and anguish?"

"It is like a heaven, isn't it?"

"Yeah, it is."

"And you'll never get it except right now, except living like this, except here, except once and for all giving up on that fucking heritage that failed you."

I let him have the last word. Eluding ourselves with this self-righteous paranoia about a conventional life is all we can afford, the only comfort we can offer ourselves.

I stop at the 7-Eleven and, except for the cashier and an old man buying milk, there is no one else in the store. It's a typical Tuesday night. I replenish my supply of cigarettes and get a minibottle of vodka to drink on the way. Back in the car, we cruise the streets. By the time we park on a side street and get out, it's already past eleven. The bouncer in front of the building salutes us with a slight nod. He searches us, and we finally pay and get in.

Inside it's dark. The music is industrial, monstrously fast and piercingly loud. I can feel Babak is already psyched up, but the first thing I do is search the dark corners for Roya. Babak motions to a woman—clad, of course, in black—across the room.

"That's not her," I shout in an attempt to be heard over the music.

"No?" he shouts back, surprised as he tries to distinguish faces across the room.

"No. She's not here. What's going on?"

"I don't know. Maybe she's sick."

"That's it, I'm leaving."

"What?" He can't tell if I'm serious or not. He can hardly hear me with the music so loud.

I'm not serious though. I'm not leaving; no one is worth that much.

I light up a cigarette and move toward my favorite spot, a corner away from the crowd but with a full view. Sparse, dim fluorescent bulbs emit the only light disturbing the darkness in the room. Underneath my black jacket, my white shirt glows like it's radioactive.

There are only a few people here. It's not even close to midnight, and this place won't be in full swing until then, but there is something amiss. Roya's absence has thrown everything off balance. She's usually there early, taking advantage of the sparse crowd and dancing by herself to the music.

"It's just our luck that Napalm isn't here," I shout to Babak as he joins me in the corner.

He nods in agreement and shouts, "The music is good though. Forget about her!"

We fall silent, and soon he moves to the middle of the dance floor. He starts moving his body to the music, twitching to the left and right and making fists at no one in particular. A security guard, a little smaller than my car and armed with an intense hatred in his eyes, spots me in the corner and inspects me under his flashlight. Once he recognizes me, he leaves me alone. His attitude, the disdain in his eyes, and the fact that he seems to enjoy what he does, reminds me of the Revolutionary Guards who spied on our every movement in tenth grade back in Iran. I'm thankful that I'm here and not there. Here I can come and go any time I want to.

Near midnight, I creep out of the corner and approach the bar. I buy a drink and try to wash the anxiety away. Then I walk to the other side of the counter so I can see the whole dance floor. I suddenly spot her in a corner. Roya is there—all five feet five inches of her—and she moves slowly to the music as she pushes streaks of red hair behind her ears. I signal Babak, who, no longer alone but with three or four other anguished faces, is making awkward moves on the other side of the dance floor. He follows the direction of my pointed finger and suddenly stops; a smile as wide as a canyon forms on his face. He starts dancing again, faster, and I feel my anxiety subside; familiar elements are falling into place; a sense of belonging is restored.

By twelve-thirty, the place is packed with people. I get another drink, light up another cigarette, and go back to my corner where two walls meet. This is the moment of beauty that I long for as I hear my favorite track play. I close my eyes, and the hard, jackhammer-like noise set to the rhythmic, pulsating beat penetrates every cell of my brain. In the dark room, a hundred figures clad in jet-black clothes jerk up and down, and the dim light barely casts their shadows on the floor. Their faces are hidden.

As a sense of solace fills me, I open my eyes, and at the other side of the room, I see the red-haired woman moving slowly to the music; she's still forcing her hair behind her ears. This woman, who, with all her efforts to quash what is Iranian in her, is my only connection to anything called home, and I'm glad she's here.

⚑ JAHANSHAH JAVID ⚔

Persia, Iowa

I just packed up and left.

When I moved to New York in 1992 I thought I had finally found a city I could call home. But four years later, I suddenly found myself unemployed and unemployable ("Wow . . . you've worked with a lot of Eye-rainian news organizations, haven't ya?"). I no longer saw the skyscrapers as magnificent works of art. They felt oppressive. That cold, blunt New York attitude was getting to me.

I called my Abadani classmate Hamid and asked him if I could crash at his apartment in Palo Alto until I found a job. No problem. My sister Iran gave me her old car, and I was on my way.

I love driving but only when I can listen to music. The car radio was broken, so I brought along my portable CD player, which I was playing at maximum volume. I had been listening to Gugush and passing through corn fields for thirty-something hours straight on Interstate 80 west when something caught my eye. I thought I saw an exit sign for "Persia." I stopped on the side of the road and drove back. I was not hallucinating.

I drove toward the town so fast, it was as if I were afraid a city of magical proportions was going to disappear at any moment. I passed more cornfields. And then there I was, in Persia, Iowa.

The town—village, hamlet?—looked deserted. There wasn't a soul around at four in the afternoon that early October day. I parked on Main Street—apparently the only street with shops. The grocery store was closed. The laundromat door had no glass. The barber shop and the café were also closed, as well as the gas station. And they weren't just closed for the day. They looked as if they had been closed for a long time and were going to stay closed for a long time to come.

The first sign of life was the minutes of a local council meeting posted behind a window of the Persia Community Hall:

August 12, 1996 . . . Mayor's Report
Discussed dogs at large. Complaints must be written for city involvement. If
[a] vicious/threatening dog [is] at large, citizens should contact sheriff. . . .

And finally, proof of human existence: the neon lights at Ray's Country Tavern across the street were on. I walked in and sat down at the bar. The bartender, a fiftyish-looking woman with short salt-and-pepper hair was playing cards with three men, two of them her age or older. Farmers.

—Hi. What would you like?

—What have you got?

—Bud Light?

—Okay.

—Glass or bottle?

—Bottle would be fine.

— . . .

—Excuse me . . . ? I'm Persian, from Iran.

—Yeah?

—Why is your town called Persia? I'm just curious.

—Aren't you the same guy who came here and asked the same question last year?

—No.

—I sent him a letter explaining everything.

—Do you have a copy of it?

—No.

One of the men joined the conversation.

—So you're from Persia, the country?

—Yes. I was passing by and thought I had to come and see your town.

—So you're Eye-rainian . . .

—Yes.

—Why do you people hate us so much?

—Well, you know, it's all politics. I don't hate you.

— . . .

—How many people live in Persia?

—About 250. It used to be 350 just a few years ago. Kids don't want to be farmers. They like the city.

—Why Persia? Do you know why your town was named Persia?

—Well, the story is that back in 1882 they were building a railway station here. One of the workers was from Persia. They named it after him. Hey Ruth! I want to buy this gentleman another drink. What would you like son?

The frozen margarita was too strong. I took a couple of sips and thought I'd better stop. I had to get back on the road. Before I left, I bought ten postcards to send to my friends. I walked out and saw a few teenagers sitting on the sidewalk. I asked them to pose for a picture and promised to put the picture on the Internet.

Another day went by. I still hadn't reached California. Somewhere in Nevada, I think, I passed a sign for "Elburz." Again, fascinated, I took the exit and turned onto a gravel road. I turned a corner on a hill, stopped, and looked as far as I could. I couldn't see anything. I thought if I got a flat tire in the middle of nowhere I might be in big trouble.

I just turned around and headed down the highway.

TARA KAI

Mother Visits

My mother came for a visit and told me I could read her mind. I wonder if it was my mind she was reading and passing it off as her own.
She said, "In those days, you were not free. You couldn't go dancing
without having your picture in the papers the next day." That was
her, telling the woman next to us in line that she used to be someone
important. "And why did you tell Timsar's wife that you had to baby-
sit? Don't tell people everything. Secrets keep you safe, remember
that."

Holding my arm, she walked along a new street she had discovered—a shortcut to the one I always took, or so she thought. "I have
two chicken in the fridge and that is good," she said. "If you have
black-eyed peas in the house, first put rice, then dill and the beans
with saffron, and you have a meal. Do you remember your father's sisters? No, you can't remember, you were small then." I said, "I remember. There was a large book of poetry in our house; it had pictures of
heroes and monsters on every glossy page. Did you bring it with you
when you left?" "Which book? I don't remember any book," she said.

"So tell me about that woman who was in a wheelchair, who was
she?" My sentences began with "so tell me about." Her stories would
not end well if she spoke of them in the past tense. "Then she got married, the poor woman, and he left her. Years later, I only saw her once,
her body was swollen, and she died shortly after," she would say. I
listened to stories, paying special attention to the tenses. That night
I dreamed of Aunt Fathi and Aunt Zahra stringing black-eyed peas
into a necklace for me.

I gave her my blue sweater, and I almost mistook her for me. My lips
were there before hers when she put on my honey-ginger lipstick.

"What do you do with those nice picture frames I send you, those miniatures?" "I have two cupboards full of ornaments," I replied. "Ornaments make good presents for westerners," she said and we left. I went through the greeting motions in my mind and thought about the position of my head before we went in. I heard her in the next room. Mother was telling other mothers whisperings of our lives; tones rising and falling with each confidential story. I greeted them and whispered into her neck, "Don't give it all away." "Isn't she an angel?" the other mother said. "These kids have an air of innocence about them that real Persians don't." "Do you remember your grandmother? She died so young, the poor woman." My grandmother was noiseless. We would walk around the house with her like flies around a bull and surprisingly she would recognize us. She would ask, "Who are you?" Like a queen, she would lie on a mattress with pillows around her, hypnotized by TV and Canada Dry.

On Saturday, I got a card from my father. "That's typical, even his birthday cards arrive on time," she said. "But you know for all he has done to me, I forgive him. I shouldn't have divorced him." Dad could utter the worst curses, but they came out of his mouth sounding clean. I looked up his number to call him. I didn't know which letter to look under—B for *Baba*? D for *Dad*? P for *Papa*? I found it under D for *Dad*. So, I did think in English after all. It has been such a long time since I spoke his language. I am a child when I speak; my hands move and my head turns to make up for the loss. I am not me.

"Let's go for a walk in the woods," I suggested. "What, a picnic?" she asked. "No, a walk," I said. "What just walk? Shall I make some food to take?" "No," I said, "people go for walks here without taking half the kitchen with them." She took us on a picnic when I was seven. White toasted bread was thrilling then. We found a small patch of grass and squeezed in between the tightly packed groups of people around us. I bit into the soft bread and sipped Coca-Cola from a can I had opened myself—just like Americans on TV. I stared at their jaws—how appetizing, how polite. Now I buy bread from a man from Afghanistan. I stare but men eat with their mouths open; they don't eat as graciously here as they did on TV.

She took some watermelon seeds on our walk. "When I see the trees and the sky I forget the world," she said putting a seed in her mouth and cracking it with her teeth. "I've been thinking about what will happen when I die. I think when I die, I'm going to see someone I love, like my mother, and she will tell me 'I am God,' and I'm shocked and happy and go with her, and I will be proud that I was with her all my life, and I didn't know it," she said, spitting out the seed. "I think about how far you've come. Look at me, I am a nobody. And the old people here are so old, they could be eighty and they're so well-dressed." "Don't spit out the seeds," I said.

A friend came to visit. I made eggplant stew and couldn't remember whether I should put whole dried limes in it. My friend ate and my mother watched. "Delicious," my friend said. "I've never had egg-plant before." "Tell her she is pretty and looks like a *zerang* girl." I couldn't translate. "Imagine that," my mother said after my friend had left, "twenty-six years old and never had eggplant before."

We watched black-and-white videos together. Girls were seduced and worked in cabarets, and men were *jahels*. "No wonder our men are chauvinists," I said. "It's just a film," she said. And we both agreed about the woman who didn't have any luck with husbands. "Change the channel and see if there are any Roman films on," she said. She, too, loved Elizabeth Taylor in *Cleopatra*. Then I changed the channel again and Forbes was climbing onto a hot-air balloon. "Look Mum, he's rich. He goes up in these balloons. Look at that elephant balloon. There's another one—a motorcycle balloon." She asked me why. "Why what?" I said. "Why does he go up in those balloons?" "He has different shaped balloons and he goes up in them," I said. "Why?" she asked again. "I don't know why," I said.

We ate chicken at a friend's house. "Such a waste. Knives and forks don't get the meat out. Can I hold it with my hand?" she asked. "Your friend has tampons in her bathroom. Everyone can see, doesn't she put them away?" she asked. I smiled at my friend and told her that my mother liked her bathroom. Once Mother gave me all her sanitary napkins and said, "Take them, I won't need them anymore." "Ask her when she is flying back," my friend said. "On the twenty-first of *Khordad*," she said. "And what's that in our date?" I asked. "That *is* our date," Mother said. "Don't eat the chicken with your hands," I said.

"I like your friend, she is polite. She dropped us off right at your doorstep. Good friends drop you off at your doorstep," she said. I don't understand her proverbs. She said, "The hand of another person is only good enough to catch a snake." I wrote it down in English. I nod when they recite poems in the middle of their conversation. I smile, I cannot react. Persian has made me speechless.

"Are you sure we're not in first class?" she asked on the train. "No, this is second class," I said. "In the airport I had to wait until the first-class passengers got on," she said. "I got on, and they were in the way. Why don't they call them last?" "I don't know," I said. "I would never fly first class if I had the money. There's no difference here," she said. "I would never pay for such big balloons." The woman sitting opposite us sucked Coca-Cola rhythmically out of a straw. Her shadow grew and reached my knees, then she engulfed me.

"Remember when you were small? You always said you would kill yourself when you became thirty." "Yes," I said. "I wanted to kill myself when you went to those secondhand shops and bought clothes for yourself." "Look at that charming man," she said. "I wonder if they get their charm from characters in films. Does life come before TV or does TV make us?" I asked. "Remember your cousin? She had the same name as those constipation pills I took, and she was always constipated. She spoke on the phone pretending she was Alexis talking to Crystal." We laughed.

My mother bought flower seeds to take with her. "They'll never grow in that climate," I said. She fried eggplants for me and left. Driving back from the airport, I listened to a cassette she had brought with her. Haideh's voice sounded good. I took the tape to my apartment. Behind the newscaster on TV was a map of the Middle East. My eyes searched for the imaginary lines beneath the Caspian Sea; it happens all the time, it's automatic. Then they showed a mosque and the sound of *Allahoh Akbar* gave me goose pimples. A friend came with a street map of Tehran and I traced my finger around names but couldn't find my street. I called my mother. "You call me long distance to ask the name of our street? You are crazy." I put a little cross on the map where our house might have been.

I wrote a letter to my mother's sister. I hadn't written since I was ten. She was my favorite aunt. I wrote in my kindergarten handwriting: "Dear Auntie, sorry I haven't written for so long" and ended the letter with "Give my regards to Reza," and then I stopped writing. I couldn't remember her second son's name. He must be twelve now. He was born after I left. So, I called my mother again, but she wasn't home.

I dreamed I was in my grandmother's house, and I was playing. The door to the guest room opened, and I went in. The two statues she had on her mantelpiece came alive and started fighting with me. I ran to my mother and aunt and told them. They took me downstairs and gave me *faloudeh*. I woke up and remembered Masod's name.

Does my aunt still think of me? Does Reza remember me? I didn't go to the post office. I turned and took the shortcut my mother took instead. And I realized that I missed her.

The Pelican

"How far is it from Tehran to the Caspian?" I ask my aunt Feri.

"Four hours," she answers, pulling the lighter from the dashboard. She takes a drag, blows smoke. "Are you comfortable, Roksi?" she asks.

"Yes," I lie, barely able to breathe in the back seat between her friends, Juju and Zeeba. My uncle Cyrus's wife, Yasmine, turns and gives me a concerned look from the passenger seat.

I remember an eight-hour nightmare with my mother at the wheel, both of us feeling nauseated and nervous, taking hairpin turns as my mother held her breath. It was perilous, and we drove slowly and carefully through twisting mountain roads, our forest green Volvo moving like a slow, safe slug.

Feri is a different sort of driver. She's a tough little bird who has us soaring through the misty morning, through fog, rain, and mountains, above the tree line where dripping wet leaves retain their bright red and yellow colors unsmudged by the rain.

"*Bism'Allah, Rahman-e-Rahim,*" Juju blesses our trip, reading from the Qu'ran. Feri is driving eighty miles per hour and fiddling with the cassette deck trying to find "Strangers in the Night." It is a steep drop if she misses a curve.

"Let's show Roksana the *Imamzadeh*," Yasmine tells Feri.

"The what?" I ask.

"Burial place of a relative of an *Imam*," says Feri.

"Don't go too fast, Feri, we might miss it," Juju says with a whine.

Juju takes her reading glasses off, leans over, twisting her entire body to put her Qu'ran away, knocking me with every move of her elbow. She is an "after the revolution" friend—what was left when university friends and co-workers at the school where Feri taught left Iran.

"The *Imamzadeh*," Juju cries, bracing herself for religion. She and Yasmine made their pilgrimage to Mecca last year together and since then have given up wearing sheer hose and observe *Ramazan*.

"Roksana, Y'*Allah*," says Yasmine, "hurry." She insists that I come to circle the tomb.

Tombs of the *Imamzadeh* are caged in metal grating, which the faithful grasp and kiss as they whisper prayers and shed tears. When the need or wish impels, a ribbon is tied around a rod of the grating and money is tossed into the tomb. There are twelve *Imams* in Shiism; the last *Imam*, a hidden *Imam* who went into concealment in childhood, has yet to come, keeping everyone on their toes.

I'm not in the habit of taking my shoes off to enter a building. An infidel, I am still lacing up my hiking boots as Yasmine and Juju, her mascara running down her tear-stained face, run back to the car.

Like the road from Boone to Asheville, North Carolina, this road is dotted with little honey and cider stands, but here there are also fresh pistachio stands and disks of *lavashak* (apricot fruit roll-ups) wrapped in plastic hanging from the awnings. The *lavashak* and honey look inviting, but, as I am learning, they are to be admired only, not enjoyed, since, according to my family, everything public in Iran is polluted and potentially dangerous.

We stop at a small stand for lunch, and before the restaurateur can offer us tea, my aunts, the germ squad, whip out their own silverware, thermos, and teacups. The only thing we accept from the man, who has placed silverware in hot water in anticipation of this paranoia, is a plate of fried eggs.

When we arrive at my uncle Cyrus's villa, Feri beeps the car horn for the caretaker, whose teenage daughter comes running. Without instruction, she helps us unpack and dusts, sweeps, and lights the samovar for tea. I am mesmerized by the sight of the twelve-foot-long curtains dramatically sweeping down from the A-shaped ceiling. The musty smell of the locked-up cabin and the seaweed waft through the air, conjuring up memories of a chilly childhood spring afternoon when I hid in these very curtains.

"Do you remember this place?" asks Yasmine.

"She was a baby," says Feri.

"Nine isn't a baby," says Yasmine.

"I remember," I say.

"What do you remember, Roksana?" asks Feri, with a smile.

"The curtains," I say.

"Oh, not these," says Yasmine. "I've had all the curtains changed twice since then!"

The caretaker's daughter places a basket of fruit in front of the fireplace. Feri brings in logs and tries to build a fire. Yasmine prepares Turkish coffee to "make our heads warm," to keep us busy.

"Turn your cup over and Juju will tell your fortune," Yasmine tells me.

"Real fortune-telling," Yasmine says to Juju. "No fairy tales."

Juju looks into my cup and tells me things we both know.

"Your father is far away. You mourn the loss of a family member. You are in love?" she gives me an inquiring look.

"No."

She dismisses my answer and quickly and forcefully reveals a fantastical future.

"You will marry; your first child will be a boy. You will travel many times, not always to Iran. You will marry between here and the U.S. Someone far away is in love with you. Be careful of cars, beware of men who love you too fast, drop those that don't. There's a dervish figure. Are you seeking religion?"

"No, I left my religion."

"She was raised Catholic," Yasmine interjects.

"What's a dervish?" I ask.

"There are two meanings, one is a Sufi, the other is a person who has Sufi qualities, who is on a spiritual path, leads a simple life."

I am amazed that I can understand this much Persian after only ten days in Iran, even Juju's fortune-telling.

Evening. Restless, my aunts decide to visit the little port town of Babol. "For food and household wares," says Yasmine, who is tireless in her pursuit of these two things. Yasmine fills her life with errands as if she's running away from something, yet compelled to stay in the same place.

My father warned me never to marry for love. He said that love is an illusion that doesn't last. He told me that only respect and friend-ship last. Love comes later, after children. Yet, Yasmine has children, and she still seems so unsatisfied. She keeps herself busy the way one keeps a light burning through the night for fear of what may happen the minute it's turned off. She is my host mother in Tehran and the only one who understands my loneliness.

When my grandmother died, my grandfather told my uncle Cyrus, who lived with him in Tehran, that he refused to return from their summer home in Damavand "until there is a woman, your wife, in that house."

On the way home from Damavand, Cyrus's Mercedes convertible skidded on the dirt road and flipped over. This brush with death left Cyrus only slightly bruised in body, but convinced in spirit that this was a sign that he should heed his father. That afternoon, in the emer-gency room of a Tehran hospital, Cyrus informed the women of the family that he would marry anyone they found for him. The women suggested my grandmother's young nurse, Yasmine. Cyrus nodded without looking up from his book.

Walking by my room Yasmine peeks her head in. I smile. She comes in and looks at my Persian text and tries to read the English translation. I help her, but she becomes impatient and leaves to do something. An hour later she brings me tea, and we try again. She's never studied a foreign language or been abroad, but she recognizes loneliness.

"Want to come on an errand? It is very boring, but if you truly think Tehran's markets may be interesting for you, please come along," she offers. She is this house's emissary to the outside—the captain of the submarine. She controls the bank accounts, the children's schooling, shopping.

"Roksana, I want to find you a boyfriend, someone who will take you out of the house, to restaurants and the park, but finding one who speaks good English for you is difficult," she says with concern.

"I don't need English, I want to learn Persian. Are you going to find Azi a boyfriend?"

"Not until she's eighteen."

"I thought Iranian girls weren't allowed to have boyfriends."

"As long as the family approves and it's just for show, for fun, to get a hamburger or go to the movies."

"What about the komiteh?"

The komiteh are the Revolutionary Guard. Decked out in green Islamic combat outfits and baseball caps (when they aren't undercover) with a patch of Qu'ranic reading, they comb the city for infidels and incubators of un-Islamic ways. They wait in the bushes and around corners to catch naughty kids and unmarried couples and chalk up a few bribes.

"To hell with the komiteh. They're too fuzule."

I look fuzule up in my dictionary—"nosey."

The air is chilly and the sky overcast. Haystacks, bundled to burn, and pumpkins are sold on the roadside. Leaves are turning yellow. Small wooden houses swoon in their solitude; it is October, near Halloween, and I think of Ichabod Crane.

An old woman in a calico chador begs at the bazaar entrance; my aunts ignore her. Yasmine moves swiftly through her errands. Juju plays bored, while Feri waits outside with Zeeba. Feri paces, smoking her cigarette, smiling at me when our eyes meet.

Buying bread is my favorite outing. The bakery is a small, boxy building with a stove and a revolving table. Before the revolution almost all bread was baked on stones in the wall ovens; now it is mechanized. This bakery is the real thing. My aunts let me stand in line for the bread, thrown at me in a hot heap, wrapped in newspapers and soot. Brushes are provided to remove dust and stones from the bread. A little girl laughs at my ineptness and instructs me in the finer points of brushing bread. Across the street a pomegranate seller operates out of the back of a 1950s pickup truck, a pitiful throne for such passionate fruit.

We return to our warm fire at the villa exhausted and hungry. Juju dances for us. Our heads are warmed. Zeeba and Yasmine are laughing; Feri watches me quietly. Even cross-legged her foot sways. They say that foot swaying is a family trait passed on by my grandmother. At my cousin Kuros's funeral my German aunt, Krista, said that Kuros did it in his baby carriage. I was reprimanded by my older aunt last week for swaying my foot. "It's not ladylike," she told me. But I notice that when Feri becomes pensive that is exactly what she does.

"Roksana, do you want to call your dad?" she asks me. She knows I'm unhappy.

I think of my first hours in Tehran; how happy everyone was to see me.

⚛ ⚛ ⚛

My uncle Cyrus, the six-foot-three-inch patriarch of the family and the owner of my late grandfather's house in Tehran, shuffles in dressed in his pajamas to greet me. I had just arrived from the airport and was exhausted. "We are very, very, very happy," he stutters in English.

His children, Azi and Ahmad, roll on the floor, laughing at his English. He chuckles at himself and shuffles away.

Yasmine and Feri waste no time beginning what will become a yearlong "mentioning" of all the various marriage prospects happily awaiting Roksana in her homeland.

"Don't worry Roksana, if there are any you don't want, I'll have them. Now, what would you like, some more food? Anything, please tell us," Sarah, my half-German cousin, asks kindly in English.

Yasmine and Feri, who can't understand our conversation, sit on the edge of their seats, leaned over, elbows on the dining-room table, waiting for Sarah to translate—to reveal what I want, how I feel, what I think.

I feel lost. My father gave me little instruction or advice. He could have told me, even if I didn't know what to ask. I thought the challenge would be the government, customs, officialdom. I made it past that in five minutes; now I'm here with my family for a year without a clue how to proceed.

The ceremony of arrival is over quickly. Alone, I become part of the creaking house, yet another being who tiptoes through silence. In the garden, to watch stray kittens, past the kitchen, where the cook shells walnuts and seeds pomegranates, past bursts of fuzzy shortwave reception from my uncle's den, and into the living room where the cuckoo clock chirps on the hour. Internal reality proceeds undeterred by social political change.

My aunts pinch my cheeks, tickle, and hug me. My role is to nod and smile, look words up in my dictionary, and, when desperate, to call Sarah. The silence that haunts my uncle's house did not come in on my heels, but I wonder if the lack of event did? Everyone is at home and idle. Surely not to baby-sit me?

My aunt Feri is an odd sort of bird-watcher; her activity is reduced to watching me and her Pakistani parrot, Mimi, sunning on the veranda. Is Feri lonely as a single woman in a culture of married women?

"Roksi, I'm teaching Mimi to say your name, Roksi, Roksi . . ."

Cyrus listens to Persian broadcasts of Voice of America, BBC, and Radio Israel while reading newspapers, magazines, and books. All the while he receives visitors. Some visitors he acknowledges, others just come to sit and stare at the wall or borrow a book. Cyrus rarely, if ever, leaves the house. I am beginning to wonder if he's really scared of the outside or just can't be bothered with it. Sarah told me that right after my uncle received a master's degree in education from the famous reformer, Isa Sadiq, he volunteered to participate in a rural teaching program in Iran's Azerbaijan province. Winter days in Azerbaijan are dark and bitter cold. On days when there was any hint of blizzard, the other teachers from the school would come to my uncle, who was in a position of respect as a teacher from Tehran, and offer to teach his class, insisting that it was too cold for him to go any distance in the snow. According to Sarah, Cyrus got in the habit of checking the clouds before leaving the house, and later, in Tehran, when he was the principal of a famous boys' high school, he would call in sick on cloudy days. I notice that he rarely bothers to even peek his head out anymore, except to water his flowers in the evenings.

Yasmine cleans all morning, even though the house is spotless. I found "help" in my dictionary the first day and asked my aunt Feri if I should help Yasmine—not that I could ever master the art of moving a straw hand broom so agilely across a Persian rug. She sweeps methodically, bent over in her peach nightgown and teal kimono, her red hair pulled back in a black velvet headband. Moving the broom like a magic wand she produces non-existent dust and lint that emerge from the intricate design of the Persian rug like magic sparks from her broom. She laughs when she catches me mesmerized. Not many succumb to the charms of her magic broom. She runs over and pinches my cheeks. I wonder how long I will retain "guest status," how long I will remain a toy, mute but aware.

The first night in Tehran, I lay alone in the wood bed in my grandfather's old receiving room, among silver coasters, glass tables, baroque-styled couches, and crystal chandeliers.

Some eleven hours passed before they woke me to tell me that my father was on the phone from the States. It was already dusk outside. The road to Asia by jumbo jet traverses at least two cycles of the earth. The conversation was dreamlike. It was too late for him to forbid me to go or warn me of the horrors of Iran, which he hasn't seen in two years. He would have come back had he not thought that it would make it easy for me—he wants me to fail, to come home where it is safe.

"No one's wearing black," I said, confused.

"They only wear black the first forty days. Sarah, Krista, and your uncle Manucher are the only ones who have to wear black for the rest of the year." I didn't mention to him that Sarah wasn't wearing black either.

He asked me how I felt. "Suddenly very American," I told him.

It's been hard to keep a smile plastered on when I feel so alone and foreign inside, a slow child in constant need of help. I know it must be frustrating for them. Their lives are tiring; my aunts come to the Caspian to escape. They wanted to bring my cousin Azi on this trip as a buffer, to entertain me, but she couldn't skip school. They want me with them, and yet they are perplexed and intimidated by the cultural and language barrier separating us. Mostly, I sit in an alcove upstairs where I can hear and see them, but they can't see me, my face buried in a book on Sufism, hoping that this alienation will pass. They take my unhappiness personally. They think that calling the States might help. My aunt Feri gives me a glance and nods at the phone. I know that if I hear my parents' voices, I'll break down. I shake my head. "Not tonight."

"Do you think that it is a person's heart, their personality, or the fact that they are family that still endears them to people they have not seen in so long," Feri asks rhetorically, after I decline to call home.

"The Qu'ran says that children don't remember feelings of love that they may have had," says Yasmine.

"You can love without remembering," says Feri.

Everyone here has an opinion on me and my memory. Is it better that I have memories of love or to start over, fresh, as an innocent, like the child I was when I left? My past is becoming myth, wrapped in a thin veil that clouds memory.

I remember playing in the family garden with my cousins Sarah and

Kuros—swimming in our pool, running in the streets, taunting the guard who stood watch at the Shah's sister's house across the street from ours. I remember my American cousins visiting from Baghdad, where my uncle was a U.S. Foreign Service Officer, and coming here, to the Caspian Sea, where I asked my father what would happen to his flip-flop sandal taken by the tide.

"It's going to the Soviet Union, Roksana," he replied. The flip-flop's journey made me realize how small the world is and yet, looking out at the sea, what a great expanse separates us.

"I can't even see the Soviet Union, Daddy, how will it get there?"

"Just because you can't see it doesn't mean it isn't there. The tide will take it."

I was fascinated by this tide that I could not see. Iran was like the sea, with an invisible tide that would carry us away.

An ominous black flag flew over the lifeguard post at the Caspian beach on overcast days when the tide was too dangerous for swimming. No black flag warned us of a change in the political tide—of revolution.

Eventually the city would be covered in smoke, a black flag that dimmed the street lights and made me scared to sleep alone at night. Too young to read newspapers, I detected a significant change in my parents; though I can't remember when one world ended and the other began. The change was as calm and as forceful as the Caspian tide, but it didn't simply happen overnight—a child would have noticed, but only one who was used to boundaries. I wasn't used to boundaries and was always wading between two worlds. When walls fell and boundaries broke, my world was little changed. Small, yet exceptional incidents that became a way of life were all that preceded revolution.

The first images are black: black chadors. My Iranian grandmother, and even my mother, sometimes wore a black chador to funerals, but this was different. Their numbers were increasing, as if preparing for the largest Shiite funeral.

Then came fists—large, angry, powerful fists, raised and punched into the air—though, for some reason, I only remember women's fists and women's voices and women's chadors pushed and crowded against our pale, peach-colored Audi as my mother drove us through Vanak Square on our way home from school.

These incidents weren't mentioned in our house. Only at night, when the electricity went off, did things change. In the evenings, I would follow my father into his room where he would turn on his shortwave radio, and we would sit silently in the dark and listen. The glowing green light would move up and down on the bass monitor to the sound of the earnest British accent—"This is the British Broadcast Corporation . . . Blistering hot, Tehran . . . The political situation became more unstable with a fire in the Rex movie theater, where the locked doors caused hundreds of deaths. The citizens are blaming the government . . . Question of revolution as thousands have taken to the streets to protest the arson."

Being here, surrounded by the physical constructions of my past, convinces me that some of my memory is true. All that time in the States—going to soccer practice and theater rehearsals, dances and movies—the memory of Iran and the images in the news loomed over me like a responsibility, a label, some sort of religion that I was born into.

Feri calls me over to her. I sit down across from her.

"Roksana, perhaps you already know, but you are very special to me, different from the rest of your siblings and cousins. Since the day you were born, you have been like my own daughter, and I want you to know that I will be a mother to you while you are here. Anything you need, come to me. I think I told you before, but I'll tell you again. There is a Qu'ran that belonged to your great grandfather. He and your grandfather wrote in it the birthdays of everyone in the family right down to Azadeh's. I want to give it to you. This Qu'ran has a curse attached to it; if harm should come its way, whoever harms it will be cursed. I held the Qu'ran to my chest when thieves broke in two months ago and wanted to take it. It's an antique, but they understood the curse and left me alone, tied up, but unharmed. It is very powerful, and you must respect it as such."

My father doesn't know about my aunt's brush with death. She asked that I keep it from him until he returns. "People abroad shouldn't be worried," she told me. Ever since then, she has slept at my uncle Cyrus's, and the Qu'ran has remained on her bookshelf at home. Why give it to me? Why not Azadeh or Ahmad? I'm not even Muslim.

I thank her; it's about all that I can say or do in this language and culture. My family's kindness and concern were not part of my expectations of this trip. The responsibility of relationships is something I never factored in. I thought that they had forgotten the little pigtailed nine-year-old who left Iran fifteen years ago. I was raised in America, where intimacy is earned and not inherited, unlike Iran where family ties are indisputable.

Early morning is the only time to buy fish in Babol. The fishermen gather to sell their catch in a makeshift market below the tiny wooden bridge in the center of town. A resplendent array of enormous white fish, fresh and smoked, awaken a ravenous appetite. The fishermen stand silently watching with their gray Caspian eyes, while younger boys run up and down the sidewalk pimping the fresh catch.

A man, not honest enough to fish, sells a baby pelican. Propped on a stool, drowning in the overflowing cloth of his brown suit, he holds the tiny animal upside down by a string strung around its tiny webbed feet. Feri is enraged but quiet as always. Her small, delicate frame gains two inches, and her speed increases as she makes her way to the pelican man.

"How much?" she demands.

"Five hundred tomans," he says.

"For this? It's a baby, there's no meat."

"OK, three hundred."

"Done," she says, handing him the money.

"Shall I break its neck for you?" he asks, still holding the pelican.

"No. How dare you sell an innocent baby bird and for a pittance? No, I don't want it killed. I'd buy more, if you had any, just to set them free," she says, delicately taking the pelican in her hands. Together we walk to the edge of the pier and find a private alcove, where Feri places the pelican in a tiny crevice between the rocks. It immediately moves up toward the place where the two rocks meet and sits still, perhaps waiting for us to leave. We stand for a few minutes, looking out at the sea. Feri asks me if I remember it here.

"You're lucky to have left," she says, now pensive.

Feri looks as though she were once a bird, small and delicate like a little robin, gentle and poised to listen, always thoughtful.

Our errands done, we go to the pier for a motorboat ride. The frosty green sea looks chilled, bottomless. I think of the remark I heard repeatedly when I first arrived in Iran, "You must be *majnun*, crazy." The eighth-century Persian poet Nezami wrote about love as a disease, a madness, in his story "Leili and Majnun." Majnun was a well-educated young man from a respectable family who fell in love with Leili, a young woman already promised to a wealthy merchant. Majnun spent his days under Leili's window reciting poetry, lamenting his forbidden love, until he was branded insane and left the town to live in the desert. He became a wandering madman. His name, Majnun, means crazy in Arabic and Persian.

Looking around the little seaside town, I sense more than déjà vu. I feel at home here and yet lonelier than ever. Maybe I am *majnun* to desire something that doesn't exist, that isn't possible. To lament loss and to live in the realm of memory is madness. But I mourn my past, the days I twisted myself up in the long curtains and hid in the folds, when I ran along these beaches, building sand castles and floating in the sea. Now the sea is segregated with an hour for women and another for men. It is as though Majnun waits under every window in Iran, poised to read the poetry of loss.

In the United States, there is a period of time after which those who have been washed away at sea are presumed dead. Memory has no such time limit. Perhaps I mourn too soon, but when something is washed away there is so little hope that it will ever return. Is that why my family hasn't mentioned my cousin Kuros? Is it too soon, or is it time to forget? Do we wait for Kuros to be memorialized, before he is allowed into the realm of memory? Will he ever really be gone? Memory returns, but only as a changed and fossilized remnant, a piece of glass that has been washed against the sand, smooth and foggy.

A chadored girl across the bank, walking home from school, makes me think of the Leonard Cohen song "Suzanne." She's a free spirit that identifies with the half-dead fish that struggle to breathe in an element that's not their own. She lets her chador fall and drag along the wet stones; her sandals carelessly wade among orange peels and fishbones, as she wanders aimlessly along the coast.

The baby pelican is no longer where we left it in the morning, hidden in the stone wall built to keep out the rising sea.

"We can only hope that it hasn't been caught again," says Feri.

The trip back to Tehran from the Caspian is long and tiring. Falling boulders and mini-avalanches have stopped traffic for miles along the steep mountain road. We sit along the roadside and drink coffee and eat sweets, chatting with the people around us. It is nice to travel as an Iranian woman. Had I come alone on a bus, I'd be gawked at and bothered, but with my aunts I am no longer the stranger taking the picture, but part of the picture itself. My colors and expressions have begun to blend with the landscape.

❀ Essays ❀

Pregnant with Sorrow

My body has been heavy with sorrow for a long time, probably as far back as the time I first heard a paternal aunt sigh and say: "Other people get sad and lose weight, not us. In our family, we *eat* sorrow. Just look at our bodies and the extra weight we all carry around." This aunt was speaking Persian and took *ghoseh khordan* quite literally. The Persian expression is composed of the noun "sorrow" and the verb "to eat." The other two aunts, who also lived with us and were privy to this conversation, did not rush in to point out her literal-mindedness. This was further proof for me that our family had a unique corporeal relationship to sorrow.

The smell and warmth of these three women's bodies were what I craved when I was sad and in need of comforting. My mother was a career woman: first a high school teacher, then a principal. In those days, my mother was fashionably thin and always professionally turned out. Her tailored dresses and suits were such a contrast to my three aunts' loose-fitting cotton shifts. While the three sisters ambled about slowly, always willing to interrupt their routine for an unannounced visit, my mother had a purposeful and quick pace.

When I came home from school, I was greeted by one or the other of these aunts' cooing, kisses, and hugs. My memory has fixed them in a sitting position on the veranda overlooking the yard or leaning over an open window combing their jet-black tresses. How I wished I had long, black hair like them and supple bodies undulating with layers of grief.

I learned from my mother that my aunts were not considered beautiful, hence their having become spinsters. Dutifully bound to literal meanings, for years I conjured up a link between the Persian word for spinster, *dokhtar torshideh* (a pickled girl), and my aunts' penchant for making huge vats of pickles. I loved their pickled eggplants and, by eating vast quantities of it, imagined I was freeing my aunts from their fate. Not that their being spinsters mattered to me. For the child that I was, they embodied unconditional love, and I was mystified by others' blindness to my aunts' perfection.

The two younger sisters did eventually marry and leave our house, but they reserved a special place in their hearts for their brother's two daughters, though it was no secret to anyone that I, the younger daughter, was their favorite. The feeling was mutual on my sister's part. She ran away from their sloppy kisses, which she washed off her face. Unlike me, she didn't jump at any excuse to race downstairs and spend evenings sitting with them on the straw mats that covered their floors.

The second story of our house where my parents, my sister, and I lived was a world apart from my aunts' quarters downstairs. We had plush Persian rugs, imposing furniture, and we slept on beds. My aunts, in contrast, had almost no furniture and rolled out their bedding on the floor every night and put them away in the morning. Unlike us, they had never replaced their clunky, loud alarm clock with the modern variety ringing out pleasant melodies. I begged to sleep downstairs where I could hear the comforting ticktock all night long.

In the world of upstairs, conversation revolved around work, school, and the hospital where my father worked. It was the world of duty, homework, education, and precision. Here language, too, seemed to work differently. My mother, especially, was fond of quoting verses of poetry in response to our questions. I was never sure if I had fully grasped the significance of her enigmatic citations. Her language was coded and far from transparent. From her, I learned the art of indirect communication and concealing layers of meaning. I wonder if that early training in interpretation is not at the root of my having developed a liking for reading and deciphering texts.

My father's speech was different. He was a man of few words, but, like his sisters, he communicated his emotions directly. Every night when he returned from work, I rushed downstairs to be the first to greet him. More than his vivacious smile, which he reserved for those he loved, his caresses on my cheeks were what I impatiently awaited. His hands always smelled of disinfectant, an odor I still associate with paternal love.

My father's return home also plunged me back into the world of responsibility and duty. He would inquire about our homework. I developed the habit of always leaving some homework unfinished so that we would have something to do together. Biology and anatomy were his strong suits. His explanations of the workings of the human body were as mesmerizing as any story I read in my Persian literature primer. The language of the body, as he related it, was far more logical and straightforward than the language of poems and prose pieces my mother explained to me. My father's voice softened the sharp edges of life upstairs.

Downstairs you entered a different time zone. Hours could be devoted to idle chatter and gossip about neighbors and relatives. I was caught between these two worlds. I knew I was expected to be a good student, get an education so that I would not sit around like my three aunts. My father took every opportunity to remind us of the importance of higher education. Any time my sister or I complained about school, he offered his sisters as examples of what would become of women who didn't acquire an education and the means to be independent. "Do you want to end up like your aunts and wash dishes for the rest of your lives?" he would say by way of shutting down further debate about the merit of memorizing reams of poetry, or tackling math problems. I knew I would never disappoint my father, but I also wanted to emulate the pace of my aunts' leisurely life and their unfailing capacity for love.

In retrospect it doesn't surprise me that I have developed a schizophrenic relationship to the work of body and mind. I did get an edu-cation and become a professional, but over the years I have let my body go the way of my aunts' bodies. I have swallowed my share of grief and transferred it into weight I carry as proof of my family her-itage. I deal with anguish by increasing my levels of consumption. The lessons I learned from my aunts have stayed with me. To their mind there was no trouble that couldn't be resolved by an offering of food. I have a vivid memory of my sorrow-eating aunt handing me a juicy pomegranate on a day when I was upset about something that happened at school. "Eat this, my child, and you'll be fine," she said. She was right: the work of peeling and digging out the juicy seeds was thoroughly therapeutic. Afterward, she washed off the pome-granate stains from my hands and face as if reminding me that my anx-ieties could be as easily rinsed away. Pomegranates are rare to come by in my new home in Canada, but there are plenty of other foods I can sink my teeth into when I feel the pangs of sorrow.

There are other childhood lessons I have incorporated into my life. To my mother's chagrin, loose-fitting cotton has remained my pre-ferred choice of clothing. Like two of my aunts, I have remained bar-ren, but I have inherited their desire to reach out to children. I have gone beyond their lesson and, when not confined by social strictures, extend my caresses to humans and animals alike. I am surrounded by cats who offer me a gentle, but aloof love. The swish of their tails against my legs, on the cold days I return home from work, is a shad-ow of the softness that enveloped me in my childhood.

This being anchored in my body has its drawbacks. Losses are so transparently written on my body I can't bear looking at myself in a mirror. The weight of sorrow shows and is sometimes beyond bear-ing. From time to time, especially when professional demands invade my peace of mind, I long to leave my body, to take all that weight off. True to my aunt's literal-mindedness, I have tried to shed the weight of sorrow by dieting and starving myself. But my body resists. After a period of successful dieting, old sensory pleasures I associate ever increasingly with food demand to be heeded. For years I have been making up for my father's and my aunts' gentle caresses by seeking pleasures of the palate. In the end, though, I am left wanting corporeal closeness and love.

Cerebral life and transcendence of the body, I have long since concluded, are not my forte. Over and over again I am returned to my body. Numerous illnesses have reinforced the immediacy of the physical: a ruptured appendix, typhoid, Malta fever, hepatitis, infected tonsils, sinus surgery, chronic joint pain, and a uterus infested with tumors make up a partial list of the battles I have fought on the corporeal front. Even when I have succeeded in stepping outside my body to gain relief from excruciating pain, I have had to confront the return to daily life, putting one slow step in front of another, and being reminded of the failings of my body. During those periods of convalescence, I have acted as any hardheaded survivor, but not without constantly being made aware of the physical reality that ties me down to a hospital bed and robs me of that noble forbearance my mother has always urged upon me. "You didn't inherit my tolerance for pain," is how she has put it on many occasions. In earlier years I used to take up her challenge and hide my pain, but, as my aunt said, it's better for us to pour our pain into our body where we feel it, if for no other reason than the possibility of some day rediscovering pleasure on that same site.

When I think of close friends and relatives I have lost, I register the pain of loss on my body. The news of a dear friend's death produced dry heaves, and the departure of a person I knew I would never see again confined me to bed for several days. I emerged from these experiences a heavier—one might even say a more rounded—person. But the picture is not yet complete. Lately, I have come to relate the absence of wholeness to the missing cadences of my childhood, to the language I first connected with love and caring. In a sense, my mind and body have not been at odds with each other. With a body bent on replicating tangible pleasures, I have been ignoring the demands of the mind not to be left out of the equation. Perhaps, like Proust, I have to realize that the taste of a certain food evokes pleasure precisely because it is linked to specific memories. Even more importantly, those memories are anchored in a particular language, history, and geography. When I reread the famous passage in *Remembrance of Things Past*, I am envious of Proust's narrator for being able to carry out his archaeological excavations in a language and location not too distant and different from the ones associated with his original experiences. Relocating my pomegranate scene in icy Canadian winters, in a second language, is somewhat more complicated. I need the sounds of Persian and the smell of the Caspian Sea to make the experience whole.

I can't eat my way back to scenes of childhood bliss. I have become impregnated with sorrow, but I also need to find a way to create something new out of what has been weighing me down. If I don't transform myself into the immaculately turned out professional woman my mother was, I would have to at least cease to couple that image with excessive control and self-denial. She too has changed. If she still sends me diets, guaranteeing quick weight loss, she has also taken to cooking and baking. On her visits to Canada, she is always in the kitchen, preparing one delicacy after another. Her culinary zeal makes me wonder if she is making up for lost time. The years my father was alive, she closely monitored his diet. As a diabetic he was forbidden sweets, though he and I snuck many an ice-cream cone when she wasn't watching. Now my mother cannot live without pastry. She is proud of her accomplishments in the kitchen and never fails to mention how much better her food is than the bland concoctions my aunts made when they lived with us. But the aunts never forbade us food. They shared everything, bland or not. Food, for them, was not a weapon. It was a means of conveying love.

In her retirement, my mother has also converted to this mind-set, but, when she offers me food now, I still remember the time I annoyed her so much with one of my questions she threw a pear she was eating at me. I don't like pears. I can't bite into them without reliving the rejection at the hands of my mother. I do relish other of Mother's food offerings. For her, too, food has become a means of salvaging missed opportunities. In my revisiting of the past, I would also have to uncover and articulate the hidden dimensions of my aunts' life histories. Why was there so much sorrow on their plate, especially when they were filled with such love? Could it be that they, too, were conscious of something missing? There is no way for me to ask them these questions. In my long-distance phone conversations with them, they repeat their sweet words of love, pray that some day I return home to see them, and then rush to hang up with their customary "I would sacrifice my life for you, dear child." When I report these conversations to my mother, she gets annoyed. "Your aunts overdo it, that expression doesn't mean anything. Who in this day and age would sacrifice herself for someone else?" My mother has never appreciated my aunts' literal relationship to language.

I might never find the answers to questions I want to ask my aunts, but weaving together their experiences and mine I can gauge the extent to which we have all transplanted psychic battles onto the realm of the physical. Concealed behind our loose outfits are traces of both sorrow and survival. The shapes of our bodies, my aunt was right to point out, are testimonials to a lifetime of not knowing what to do with our corporeal selves. A doctor recently told one of my aunts that she needed to lose weight. To persuade her of potential health risks, he told her to think of her excess weight as equal to two large suitcases she was condemning herself to carry everywhere. I am not sure the metaphor helps. Who would want to lose the contents of those suitcases? The doctor is obviously of a different genetic makeup. He doesn't understand about eating sorrow. Had he offered my aunt a new expression, one dealing with eating joy and losing excess weight, she might have taken his medical advice more seriously. In the absence of such a turn of phrase, my aunts and I are left struggling with our oversized bodies, though these same unruly shapes are attuned to the most intricate nuances of affection. Our bodily salvation may well lie along a different path of self-expression. After all, wasn't it in the folds of my aunts' aggrieved bodies that I found the most enduring experience of human warmth and attachment?

Perhaps the day I rewrite this piece in Persian and offer it to the four women who have shaped the paradoxes of my corporeal being, I will find a new way of handling the bundles of sorrow I wear on my body.

NAZANIN SIOSHANSI

The Suffocating Sense of Injustice

Walking among the white marble graves of my predecessors, I finally feel at home in Iran. It is these silent pillars of a minority people that provide me with a sense of belonging; these buried bodies are a stronger connection than the hustling bodies outside of the cemetery gates. I am standing at the physical end point of my race and can now see full circle.

Our minority status within the Islamic population became painfully obvious during our midmorning drive to Tehran's only Zoroastrian cemetery located in the southernmost district of the city. Coming down from the north with my mother and uncle, I watched as houses and apartments grew shabbier, as elegant black silk and cotton clothes shifted to sweat-soaked polyester attire. In the streets, the smell of gasoline, dust, heat, and bodies became overwhelming. Soon, the commotion of the roads became so overwhelming that they rocked me to sleep.

I awoke to silence. We had passed the last inhabited area of the city. The silence was eerie. All around us were dried fields closed in by barbed-wire gates. We could see no one except for the sentry standing at attention on some raised platforms. In the distance, dormitory-like buildings seemed to rise from the dust. While piecing together this imagery, I sensed my uncle's tension. He moved closer to the wheel, anxiously looking out of the window as if to spot something or someone. Finally, in a low voice he whispered, "Cover yourselves well, ladies."

Four men came up to the car, demanding that we stop. No warning was given. We were obviously below them. The men surrounded our car. Two of them stood near my mother and me and looked at us with

239

such intensity it felt as if they were touching us with their eyes. Another man was circling the back of the jeep.

The man at my uncle's side yelled with angry self-importance, "What's your business?" It came out as a squawk.

In an even voice, my uncle replied that we were going to the cemetery half a mile down the road. I could feel the men beside us looking at us. "Heathens," their Muslim eyes seemed to say as they surveyed our clothing. After all, we were going to the cemetery dressed in yellows and purples.

Finally, the man at my uncle's side acquiesced. Words were too much of an effort, so he just threw his head back and flared his nostrils. One of the men turned and spat as we drove past. His message was clear.

No one spoke. We parked down the road. I got out behind my mother and looked at the mulberry trees that provided a second gate to the wire one behind them. As we entered the cemetery, a family dressed in black was exiting.

It was then that my mother broke down and muttered angrily, "They've reduced us to wearing black. Those low-class . . . And them," she said, pointing to the family we had just seen, "do they call themselves Zoroastrians? Wearing black to see their dead? Is that the respect they pay? Breaking tradition and religion . . ."

My uncle just shook his head with disgust. "They begrudge us visits to our land, to our own ancestors, every time. The land they stand on, that they conduct their military exercises on, was supposed to be a place of peace. The *Sepah* is making this cemetery their mock battleground."

The *Sepah*: fabled words of doom. I'd heard of this fourth branch of the military—full of only the most ardent supporters of the Islamic Republic. It was ingenious of Khomeini to form it. The revolution came about, in part, because of dissension within the Shah's military ranks. This new arm of the military was intended to quash any disloyalty, and many members of the original revolutionary circle were rewarded with positions within it. The unused acres of the Zoroastrian cemetery were confiscated for the sake of their revolutionary fervor.

Both my mother and uncle relaxed when they saw the caretaker, a little old man in a navy suit. As he spoke, his few yellow, cracked teeth became visible. His rough brown skin was etched by years of working in the sun. Welcoming us in a thick, ancient accent, he asked how my grandmother was. It was this recognition that made Tehran my mother's home.

I followed behind, observing the different shapes and styles of the tombs as we moved from distant ancestors to the more recently buried. I don't think I have ever been among so many Zoroastrians in my life. My mother instinctively found her way to her father's tomb. She poured the rosewater she had brought over it, feeding his grace with the sweet fragrance. My uncle then began reciting a holy verse from the Avesta (the ancient Zoroastrian holy book). The others joined in as if they were expressing some internal and natural rhythm they learned in childhood. The sounds of the words, the smell of the rosewater, and the cemetery stretched out in front of me made everything feel complete and harmonious. It could not have been any other way. There was no hyphenated identity here. An Iranian-American, with both sides fighting for dominance, did not exist. I joined the chorus of chants.

Later, I became contemplative and left the others to be alone. Everything seemed natural here—religion, identity, and place. At home, in the States, it was so different. At my paternal grandfather's funeral service held at a large, beautiful hotel in California, there was no peace like this. The modern, sterile ballroom where we held the service did not afford the same sense of return. It was the last slight given to an exile.

I gave the eulogy at my grandfather's funeral. My father and uncle also spoke, but neither of them knew how to convey the important experience of loss that my grandmother wanted to be told.

I had no tears or remorse for my grandfather's inevitable death. He had suffered from Alzheimer's disease for five years. Holding my grandmother's hand as she wept silently, I listened to my dad give a factual outline of his father's life. Then my uncle stood and told some stories, adding color to the sparse, puritanical life story my father had told. And then came my turn.

I looked out at the audience of mourners. In the wave of black-clad Muslims and Christians, the Zoroastrians stood out in their white clothing. "We mourn in white and other light colors," my grandmother had emphatically told all of her nieces and nephews. "It is our tradition." To wear black would not be to succumb to death, but to the traditions of the majority religions.

With this moment of introspection I had captured the attention of my entire audience. The story I was about to tell was the tale of every exiled person, the tale of dislocation from the natural progression of a life.

"I stand before you to tell you a tale that my father would not tell and my grandmother could not tell. It is a tale that every relative, friend, and acquaintance of my grandfather's should know. It is a tale about a fellow being's desires, losses, and the injustices they've suffered.

"A couple of years ago, before my grandfather became a victim of Alzheimer's, he and my grandmother were watching the evening news, passing time in their usual fashion. During the broadcast there was a story about the death of an important military official. This man's name and nationality does not matter. Bereavement is universal. My grandfather stared intently at the screen, watching as the coffin was carried with the nation's flag draped over it, noting the generals who followed in descending rank, each carrying a pillow with the deceased's medals and stars pinned onto it. When the video clip was over, my grandfather fell momentarily silent. Then quietly he turned to my grandmother and with serene dignity said, 'That is the only thing that I am sorry to have lost. When I die no one will give me such a ceremony.'

"With those two lines he finally voiced his most personal anguish. He told us what we already knew. He did not care about the land or money that he left behind. What he had lost was something that could not be replaced—the recognition of his life's work, the recognition of his identity. He entered the army as a young man, and through hard work and determination he became a three-star general. It was a rare and widely respected feat to have achieved such a high position in Iranian society.

"And so I relate this story to you. It is we, his family and friends, who must remember him for what he did in his life, in an era that no longer exists for him or for us. After the revolution, there was blatant injustice; innocent victims were hurt by others' corruption, but there was also blatant injustice before the revolution. We must bow our heads to these incidences of pain and wrongdoing.

"It is in relation to my grandfather that most Iranians recognize me. As his granddaughter I will work all my life to tell his tale, to prevent him from being forgotten. My greatest sense of pride comes from being the granddaughter of Major General Khodamorad Sioshansi."

And with that conclusion, I stood a moment longer behind the podium. Then I walked away quietly to sit next to the *mobed* ("priest"). I was aware that the room had filled with applause, and that many in the crowd were crying—touched especially by my last sentence. To a degree, they were crying for themselves. Our family names no longer carried the same weight in American society. Their tears were not only for the loss of a friend, but for the loss of a history, a place, and their connection to that place.

As I walk among the other graves, I imagine my grandfather's tomb here. I remember the pain that followed the days following his death in July of 1994. Many high ranking military and government person-nel sent extravagant flower arrangements, but didn't show them-selves at the service because they were afraid of undercover spies. No family members were willing to conduct a service in Tehran. To bury the only three-star Zoroastrian general since the Persian Empire a mile from the revolutionary *Sepah* headquarters would have been an insult my family could not have countenanced. I soothed myself by sit-ting and imagining his tomb here among the others and how a cere-mony for him here would have been conducted.

Yet dreams of a changed past do not ease a present painful reality. I can build imaginary scenarios between the white marble and the mulberries, but the relief it offers is as short-lived as a bubble. I am an Iranian-American, displaced from my origins.

A few nights ago we drove by our old house with my father's best friend. Rather spontaneously he said, "Remember how we hid the General's medals behind the water heater in the attic? God, there was less than a foot between the heater and the wall. We had to scale the inside of the chimney to enter from the inside maintenance door."

I grew excited at the thought of the medals. Butterflies flew around in my stomach. But my face also revealed a deep anguish. Slowly, my mother turned and stared at me. "Sorry," she whispered, answering my unspoken question. Her eyes were telling me there was no way to retrieve those medals. It was too dangerous, physically and politi-cally. She looked away. I stuck a fist deep inside my mouth while I dug the nails of my other hand into the flesh of my palm, containing a cry too deep and inconsolable to voice.

SIAMAK NAMAZI

Finding Peace in the Iranian Army

I will never forget boarding that plane. I was finally going back to the land I had practically fled from at the age of twelve. I had no clue what to expect, but the six-hour layover in Kuwait certainly had my imagination going. I stepped onto the airplane on final call, knowing that this was the last chance I'd have to change my mind.

My parents had urged me not to join the Iranian army and even offered to pay for a military exemption. Military service for Iranian males over the age of eighteen is mandatory, but most who have been living abroad since childhood chose to pay for an exemption. My parents, however, seemed to understand that I considered buying an exemption socially unjust and unacceptable.

When I arrived at Mehrabad Airport I became anxious and filled with questions. Would they question me at passport control? Would they give me notice to report for service immediately? To my surprise, the officer said nothing and waved me on toward customs. "Do you have any foreign goods?" asked an old, ill-humored man. "I left when I was twelve, so some of me is bound to be foreign," I said trying to joke with him. He looked at me flatly and waved me through the line. At the exit, a few dozen relatives stood smiling behind the glass and rushed to greet me as I cleared customs.

For a few months, I was in a complete daze. I could not remember the names of most of the streets or even the names of half of my distant relatives. After a few weeks, I began to think about my next step. I insisted on going to the draft office by myself. "I have come here to learn about Iran. I have to face the bureaucracy and its problems if I want to learn how to improve it," I would say to offers of help. My relatives laughed at my stubborness but let me be. Well, most did, and the rest I politely ignored.

While I expected obstacles, I never imagined it would be so hard. First, my birth certificate dated from the Shah's time and was no longer valid. So I had to change that. Then I headed to the draft office to register. After waiting in a line for two hours, I entered a room occupied by a colonel. I enthusiastically introduced myself and my plans only to hear: "Why are you saying all this to me? I'm not in charge of such affairs. You're in the wrong room. Get out!" It took an hour just to find out who I needed to talk to and what I needed to do. I discovered I had to have the authenticity of my university degree certified in the States, then give it to the Ministry of Education for evaluation, and only then could I register. A couple of months passed just waiting for these documents to be processed.

While sorting out that mess, I learned that I could fulfill my military service by working for a university or government agency. The university or agency interested in hiring me would have to request a mandate from the Commander-in-Chief's Office that would allow me to serve my duty in this way. But things are never as easy as that in Iran. A lot of people gave me advice and everyone introduced me to anyone they thought could help. Slowly, I made a list of agencies and went door-to-door, or rather, contact-to-contact. Some places brushed me off but most had me come in and talk, which is not surprising since their friends had referred me to them.

I learned that to obtain work with a government agency, a division within that agency had to submit a request for my employment to their Deputy Minister. Chances of employment ride on the relationship between the person who submits the request and the Deputy. If the request is granted, that Deputy writes to another Deputy who is in charge of "Draftee Affairs" and the process goes on—and on. After a string of further approvals and requests, the Ministry finally sends an official request to the Commander-in-Chief's Office. This is just the tip of the bureaucratic iceberg. The hardest part is getting the approval of this office.

Having worked in Cairo for an international nongovernmental agency after my graduation from Tufts University, I had learned never to leave any documents with people, as the papers would very likely go astray. And so, not trusting others to push my paperwork along, I was searching for one official or another with my file in hand when I got lost in the *harasat* wing (the security wing responsible for enforcing Islamic codes). I asked a young bearded man where the *gozinesh* office was—the office whose approval I needed next. Typical of an Iranian, he started asking me curious questions. Before long, he took my entire file and read it, and we had a nice conversation about returning from abroad. He seemed to enjoy my unusual story and simply could not believe I had returned to Iran when my parents were not even there.

Now that we were such good friends, I asked him what the *gozinesh* was all about. I was horrified to learn that it is a selection board that tests applicants on their knowledge of Islam; which position I would be eligible for depended on how well I did on the test. My new friend told me not to worry, though, as he would arrange for me to meet an old college buddy of his who was on the board. I didn't chance it and began studying ten days before the test. Luckily, I was asked very simple questions and was told it should not be a problem. Two weeks before my draft date, after everything for my mandate had been processed, I learned that I had failed the ideology test! With the help of my friend's college buddy, however, I managed to talk my way out of this predicament by pointing out that although I had been living in the United States for many years, my knowledge of Islam was still considerable. At last, my mandate for a position at the Ministry of Housing came through.

The day I received my draft papers, I entered a building in which each room corresponds to dates of birth. In the room for my birth date, I gave my name and *shenasnameh* (birth certificate) number. I was in the middle of telling the attendent that there was no way he would find my name in any of the hundreds of binders that occupied the shelves of the room, when he found it. It took less than a minute. How was it that my name was in this God-forsaken building that until that moment I thought of as an unorganized zoo? It was very unsettling.

Not surprisingly, Iran's draft process proved to be very disorganized and disorienting. I was given a piece of paper and told to report to *Padegan-e Vali Asr* (a military post) on the draft date; there, the draftees are assigned to either the army or the *Sepah* (Revolutionary Guard). When the day finally came, I was wandering with a crowd of other clueless, lost draftees, looking for the right place at 5:00 A.M. Some people had bags with them, not knowing if they would have to go that day as their service had officially started. I was assigned to the army and told to report to another building in eight days. Eight days later, still not expecting to be taken, I found myself searching for another military base in Tehran. There, the draftees were further divided among ground, air, and naval forces. I was assigned to the ground forces, which, as my luck would have it, required the longest training. I was to suffer six long months before going to the Ministry of Housing. Next, they took us to our station and divided us into platoons and companies. Then, we were given some clothes with no regard to size and told how to sew on the various badges. We were also given the name of the district in Tehran where we could have the clothes altered for a fee. In five days' time, we were to report for training in properly fitted clothes and with shaved heads.

Time passed and it was almost time to report for boot camp. One day, I was sitting at a gathering, drinking *aragh sagee* (strong vodka), when I decided it was time I had my hair shaved off. Women didn't see me as much of a catch after that, especially as the having-returned-from-abroad thing had already worn thin. In any case, I believe that on that day I became the first graduate of Tufts' Peace and Justice Program to wear the army gear of the ground forces of Iran.

Nothing is as scary as entering boot camp. It started in the middle of *Ramazan* and winter. I wondered if I should tell everyone about having lived abroad. It all came out rather quickly, though. The first line of conversation generally began with a question about where and what I had studied. And what wasn't revealed in conversation was revealed in the forms we were required to complete. I thought I was going to be in a lot of trouble answering some of the questions truthfully like, were any members of your family part of the former regime? Truth is, I was received with curiosity mostly. If anything, I was treated more nicely for having come from abroad.

What I did not know and was not happy to learn was that there are written exams in boot camp. Guess how I felt about taking notes on military tactics and equipment given the state of my Persian! I was also horrified to learn that I would have to attend Islamic ideology classes. But to be honest I valued these classes the most. No one in the military treats you as well as the *mullah* who teaches that class. If you doze off in any other class, be prepared to run around the grounds or something; in ideology class, on the other hand, the *mullah* doesn't care if the entire class lays their head on the table and sleeps. And that's exactly what we did.

One of the most valuable lessons I learned while in boot camp took place outside the walls of the base. One day I managed to get a half day's leave on a day that all leaves were canceled by order of the general. I headed toward my uncle's house in Sa'adat Abad and a nice hot shower. In my state of happiness, I longed to share my joy with others. There was an older lady, about sixty or so, in the last taxi I took on my way to Sa'adat Abad. I complimented her on her perfume, just to make her day. Instead of a thank you, she responded with "*khejaalat bekesh!*" ("shame on you!"). I tried to explain, but the screeching of the brakes suggested that I was failing to do so. As I gasped for breath

some distance away, I recalled that just weeks earlier similar statements drew a *"lotf dareed shoma Agha"* ("you are very kind, sir").

What I learned that day is that your rights in Iranian society are
completely defined by the social class you are believed to belong to.
Before boot camp, when I was still in my American Levi's jeans,
Tehran was a very different city to me. More accurately, I was a very
different person to Tehran. I recall days I spent riding in shared taxis
so I could reacquaint myself with the city and listen to what people
were saying and thinking about life in Iran. It was almost written on
my forehead that I had just recently returned from abroad. Iranians
are not known for their ability to restrain their curiosity either. They
would talk to me, ask questions, and treat me, well, like a young educated man just back from the States.

What escaped me on the day I was rejoicing all the way to Sa'adat
Abad was that I looked very different now and was perceived differently. In my dirty gear, with buzzed hair, and no stars on my shoulders to indicate education (stars are awarded upon graduation from
officer training), I was a plain, uneducated soldier, most probably
from a rural background. If a woman accidentally brushed against me
as I passed through the crowded streets, it was I who rubbed up
against her. I learned the hard way that I no longer had the right to
engage in familiar talk with everyone.

All this came to me in less than a second as I pushed open the door
of the taxicab and ran as fast as I could after hearing the taxi driver
pull up his handbrake angrily. I knew it wasn't a friendly gesture. It
was a good experience, though—a lesson I still carry with me.

After boot camp, I was stationed in Shiraz for officer training. Unfortunately, the ground forces do not provide transportation. They
simply give you a little compensation money, which you receive four
to five months later. I bought a plane ticket not knowing how I would
find the base in Shiraz; I only knew the name of the barracks and nothing about the town. Fortunately, everyone knows where these places

are in smaller cities. After three months in Shiraz, Tehran seemed like an amalgam of Paris, New York, and Los Angeles.

A few weeks before training ended, I asked someone to make sure my mandate was in order. It wasn't. There are so many tales in the army about these mandates. Your superiors tell you they can revoke it, but it doesn't make sense that a lower body can challenge the authority of the Commander-in-Chief's Office. After every step, I was told it was now final and definite, only to encounter some new problem. In Iran, nothing is finished until it is finished.

Being in Shiraz was stressful; I didn't know what would become of me. If the mandate didn't come through, I would be classified according to my status—both familial and educational. I did well on my exams, but still, given that those who are only sons have first choice, I could hope for Kerman—a base in the middle of a desert— at best. The two hours it took to announce the final assignments seemed like an eternity. My name was the very last one on the roll of people whose mandate had arrived. It was a great relief, but I was also sad as I had met the most beautiful girl in Shiraz. We would see each other in the restaurant of the Homa Hotel, where I hoped the *komiteh* (local revolutionary organizations) would have less of a presence. There, we would sit and talk for hours among the tourists. To think what they would have done to me if they caught me dressed in a soldier's uniform! I once actually forged a signature to get off base to meet her.

After I completed officer training in Shiraz and returned to Tehran, I had to deal with a new host of bureaucratic messes: the Ground Forces Headquarters could not find my mandate, which I had hand-delivered there. They wanted to assign me to some base, God knows where. After much frustration, perseverance, and luck, my mandate finally did come through.

It took a few weeks to recuperate and to shed the paranoia and mis-trust that had been instilled in me. I rented an apartment in Shah-rak-e Gharb and started working at the Ministry of Housing as a civilian. I was back to being the young man who had recently come back from the U.S. I had my own apartment, my hair grew back, and I regained my lost social status—and perhaps learned to milk it bet-ter as well. I came to know the hidden night life of Tehran and made some good friends.

But I also lost a lot. The CDs I had a diplomat friend bring from my collection in Cairo, the satellite dish my new neighbor had, the pic-tures in my apartment of my friends and family abroad, and an array of other normal items meant that I now had to be cautious. I had to build an invisible wall and be discriminating about whom I let into my apartment and whom I did not. I could no longer associate with everyone and anyone, regardless of whether they were *Hezbollahi* (re-ligious partisans of God), *motadayyen* (believers), or *bacheh-gherti* (punks). It is not about snobbery—it is about surviving in a society of *komiteh* and *amr-e beh ma'roof* (the enforcment of Islamic ethics), where owning a simple videotape of a PG-rated movie can be a crime. Like every other Iranian, I learned to have two faces: one for inside the walls and another for the outside world. I created a subsociety within the Islamic Republic where I could express my opinions freely and with little worry of the consequences. I had free speech, but only within the confines I created.

I would try to meet my conservative friends from the army outside; those who were part of the *Basij* (the revolutionary military) came from religious backgrounds. But eventually I got tired of making ex-cuses to get out of having them over. I got tired of the guilt. So, my pool of army friends was reduced to two. I had learned a wealth of lessons from them, and they taught me more about Iran than any of the classes I sat in on at Tufts. These friends were lost to me. I still think about them.

The two and a half years I spent in Iran are marked by some of the best memories of my life. In Iran you are either in heaven or hell. There are very few in-betweens. I miss it now. Boot camp and officer training, although rigorous, served as the best classroom I could imagine to reintroduce me to Iran. I was able to live with and get to know Iranian youth in a setting that overcame Iran's strong class and ideologically segregated system. The entire mosaic of Iran was present—Persians, Azeris, Kurds—and I was exposed to experiences no internship could provide. Most importantly, I found peace within myself. My return to Iran made me appreciate all the basic comforts and freedoms I have in the United States, many of which most Iranians are deprived of. It certainly put life in perspective.

Even with the restrictions and all the problems in Iran, I still loved living there. Aside from the smog and pollution, the view of Damavand still evokes more feelings within me than I can express on paper. A hopeless romantic, I do feel the spirit of Arash (one of Iran's legendary epic heroes) there. Isfahan is half the world for me, and Shiraz is the most poetic city in the world. No restaurant in any of the continents I have visited has ever been able to match the experience of sitting on a bed in Darakeh and having *jigar va mast* (liver barbecue and yogurt) under the shade of its magnificent trees.

Most of all and by far, the warm, emotional, and beautiful people of my motherland are irreplaceable for me. They taught me what friendship means, what family means, what having roots means. I left Iran a child of twelve and returned a young man of twenty-two. But to my uncles, aunts, cousins, and extended family, I was still Siamak. They gave me their unconditional love and support—immediately. They showed me what it means to have a home. Even if I never return, I know that if someday my children were to visit Iran, they would be granted unconditional and limitless love, just because they are my children.

And so, when I decided to return to the United States and pursue a master's degree, my heart was full of sadness. Although my tears fell uncontrollably as I said farewell to all my loved ones, I left knowing who I was and what it means to be Iranian.

If anyone has the crazy idea of returning to Iran without paying off the Islamic Republic and has questions, feel free to contact me.

⚔ FEREYDOUN SAFIZADEH ⚔

Children of the Revolution: Transnational Identity among Young Iranians in Northern California[1]

More than a decade ago, Robert Cole argued that a nation's politics becomes a child's everyday psychology.[2] How true this is with respect to many Iranian children who came to the United States as children of immigrants, refugees, exiles, or asylum seekers in the aftermath of the 1979 Revolution in Iran. These children have lived not only with the displacing effects of that revolution and their immigration, but also with the fallout from the tense political relations between Iran and the United States. Many of their parents, themselves struggling with the impact of displacement, have not been able to have an impact on international and local politics. Furthermore, both the children and their parents have been swept into the middle of the multicultural identity politics of the 1980s and 1990s here in the United States.

For the most part, parents do not know how their children experience, understand, and perhaps resist or reshape the complex, frequently contradictory cultural politics that inform their daily lives. Many children with Iranian backgrounds must move in and out of diverse roles and create identities that often bewilder and trouble their parents. These children are struggling with numerous and often contradictory identity claims, and their minds have become "the terrain for adult battles."[3]

Cultural and identity reformulation by young Iranians invites anthropological study. The stories of a number of my students at the University of California at Los Angeles, San Francisco State University, and other schools, as well as my knowledge of anti-Iranian feelings and activities on a number of university campuses in California, first brought this subject to my attention. For example, while discussing diversity and multiculturalism in an anthropology class, a tall and athletic twenty-year-old man said, "I did not realize how malicious young kids can be," and went on to describe his memories of being beaten by a number of his fifth-grade classmates and the fear that it brought to his daily life. This student was harassed for two years and was occasionally beaten by ten- or eleven-year-old children in response to the media's portrayal of events in Iran. This young man's mother was an American. Another case involved a woman who, as third and fourth grader, had been harassed and even hit in the schoolyard and on her way home. The difference in her case was that an American classmate had often defended and protected her. The recollection of vivid details and the consensus that these experiences had indelibly affected their sense of self and identity as children and as Iranians was striking.

The experiences of these students and the anti-Iranian attitudes I encountered elsewhere made me aware of how little we know ethnographically about the lives of Iranian children who were suddenly thrown into mainstream America because their parents moved here or decided not to return to Iran. By and large, these individuals ranged from ages five to eighteen and were in Iran or in the United States or somewhere in between when the revolution took place in 1979. Since that time, they have grown up in the midst of an unusually turbulent climate generated by the politics of Iran, the revolution, the hostage crisis, the Iraqi attack on Iran, and the continuing strained relationship between the United States and Iran. The taking of U.S. hostages at the American embassy in Tehran in November of 1979 and the intensive media coverage of this event precipitated many strong reactions against Iranians in this country. Some of these reactions were directed against young Iranians.

Equally distressing are the attitudes and remarks of some parents and other older Iranian immigrants, including teachers of Persian, toward young Iranians. Disparaging comments are made about their ability or inability to speak Persian, their accent, and their American mannerisms. It is not uncommon to hear some Iranians say, "These children are not Iranian, they don't know who Hafiz, Sa'di, and Ferdowsi are. They cannot read poetry, they don't understand what love means in the work of Omar Khayyam." Their dismissals are often sharp, harsh, and arrogant. This is especially disturbing because the expectations and needs of the parents and other adults with whom these children interact shape to a large degree their Iranian and emerging Iranian-American identity.

Studies of immigration in the social sciences often focus on the structural aspects of the phenomenon, such as the economic, political, and religious factors that induce people to immigrate, as well as the ways in which immigrants interact with the host society. Individual and personal accounts of this experience have received little attention. Only recently have social scientists, particularly anthropologists, begun to examine these accounts. As a contribution to this literature, I videotaped a series of group discussions among Iranian-Americans that would serve as a record of the comments and behavior of the participants; I hoped that these discussions would help shed light on the experiences of immigration and identity among Iranians.[4]

Existing ethnographic evidence, which indicates that people with diverse backgrounds are communicating surprisingly well with one another about their experiences and identity construction in this country, was very encouraging. Regardless of their sex, the time of their arrival in the United States, their familiarity with the English language, and whether they belong to different ethnic, religious, class, and linguistic groups, they succeed in communicating many complicated concerns with great effectiveness and often have pro-foundly meaningful interchanges. I hoped to capture such conversa-tions during these video sessions. The sessions would also provide an excellent means of exploring how Iranians living abroad, particularly in the United States, discuss personal, ethnic, national, and transna-tional identity.

More importantly, these video sessions—selections of which are transcribed below—were envisioned as forums in which immi-grants, exiles, refugees, and asylum seekers could speak out for them-selves and share their personal stories and experiences. The selections provide a sampling of the issues that are of concern to many Iranians who are living in this country. Even as U.S. citizens, they are still so-cially, culturally, and psychologically forging personal identities that resonate differently with a variety of backgrounds.

Those who participated in the videotaped discussions were sepa-rated into two groups. First, I spoke with younger Iranians with lit-tle or no experience or memory of Iran. Discussions focused on sense of self, their dual and multicultural backgrounds, and identity. Sec-ond, I interviewed individuals with much stronger memories and per-sonal connections to Iran. With this group, discussions were mainly reflections on their present life in the United States and how life here compares with life in Iran.

Although these transcripts are a written record of the videotaped sessions, they do not capture the complex nature of these conversa-tions. Nonverbal forms of communication—body language, the pres-entation of self—are lost in the transcription and the translation of the participants' statements. The written word is a powerful com-munication tool; its limitations are nevertheless evident when it is used to convey all the nuances of meaning that inform a spoken dis-cussion.

General topics that emerged from the video sessions ranged from language as a gateway to experiencing a culture, cultural and ethnic boundaries, and crossing these boundaries to gender differences in the experience of immigration, politics of the homeland, and the immigrant's place in a host country. Each of these and other related subjects have been explored in great detail by scholars. However, most of these topics underpin many of the everyday concerns recent immigrants, exiles, refugees, and asylum seekers have. They also address the key issue of being caught between two cultures, of being a "halfie," neither here nor there, which can be crippling, but which can also be a source of emancipatory power. I would argue it is often the latter in the case of many young Iranians.

NOTES

1. Arlene Dallalfar, Mehdi Bozorgmehr, Alison Feldman, and Kaveh Safa read an earlier draft of this paper and offered insightful comments. My special thanks to the participants in the April 8, 1996 seminar at the Center for Middle Eastern Studies/Committee on Iranian Studies, Harvard University, and the Hagop Kevorkian Center for Middle Eastern Studies, 17th Summer Institute, New York University, June 12, 1996, who also offered thoughtful comments on an earlier draft of this paper.

2. Robert Cole, *The Political Life of Children* (Princeton: Princeton University Press, 1986).

3. For an examination of the ways in which children are central figures in contemporary debates over the definition of culture, its boundaries, and significance see: Sharon Stephens, ed., *Children and the Politics of Culture* (Princeton: Princeton University Press, 1995). See, in particular, her introduction: "Children and the Politics of Culture in 'Late Capitalism'," pp. 3–48.

4. The research and video sessions were completed in San Francisco and Berkeley during the fall of 1993. I would like to thank all the individuals who participated in the discussion sessions. I am also grateful to Farhad Kalantari for his cinematographic and organizational assistance.

Videotaped Sessions

SESSION 1

From a session with three undergraduate female students at the University of California, Berkeley. My questions appear in italics.

Ms. E ✖ I was born in Tehran, and we moved when I was four or five to London. We stayed there five and a half years and then we moved to Toronto. We lived in Canada for four and a half years. After that, we moved here, and we have been living here in California for seven years this coming August. We came to California in 1986 or 1987. We came here when I was fifteen or sixteen. I was going to be a sophomore in high school. We have family here, but the majority of my family is back in Iran still. We also have family in Europe, Los Angeles, and my cousin has lived here for thirteen, fourteen years now. We came here to be together, we did not have any family in Canada. My older brother went back to Iran and got married, but my other brother and parents are here. My father's business is back in Iran. So, basically he travels all the time. I went to Northgate High in Walnut Creek. It was hard for me to make the adjustment from Canada. Toronto was more international and diverse. I wanted to be a dental hygienist, so I got my certificate from a dental school in San Francisco. Then, I went to Diablo Valley College and transferred to UC Berkeley. I changed my major. This is my last year at Berkeley, and I want to go to nursing school after finishing. I think it would be very hard for me to move back to Iran and live there after having grown up in London, in Canada, and here for many years. I just don't think I could really adapt to that kind of life. But I am interested mostly in going back to visit my family, to see my aunts and cousins, and to visit everybody. My cousin is going to Iran tonight. I almost went there a couple of years ago. She is in high school and goes back all the time.

Ms. A ✄ I was born in Daly City. I spent the first two years of my life in Pacifica and have lived for seventeen years in Sunnyvale. My dad's side of the family is from Iran. He came thirty years ago. My mom's side of the family is from Nicaragua, although she was born and raised here in San Francisco. I have never gone to Iran, but I would like to, and my dad has not gone since he has come. We have pretty much a lot of family in this area—Sunnyvale, Foster City—on my dad's side. But the majority of his family is still in Iran. My dad's mother lives with us. She is from Azerbaijan, from Baku. She speaks Turkish, Russian, and Persian in the same sentence. My dad has two brothers. They have their own family and children. He also has an uncle in Los Angeles. One brother married a Persian woman and the other a Norwegian woman. My dad talks a lot about his family in Iran, and I have seen pictures of them, so I would like to go and see them. On my mom's side, we have family in this area also, but not much, mostly in Nicaragua. I also would like to go to Nicaragua. I went to Homestead High School in Cupertino, and I like it there; it is a good school. Then, I went De Anza College and transferred to Berkeley for my junior year. I am going to go to law school and want to be a civil rights lawyer.

Ms. B ✄ I moved here when I was small. Seventeen years ago, two years prior to the revolution. We moved here with my father, mother, and sister and have stayed in the Bay Area since. First, we moved to Pennsylvania and then to Berkeley. I don't actually have a lot of relatives here. I have a cousin in Los Angeles, and my other cousin is in South Carolina. We bought a house here, and my father has taken a couple of trips to Iran, and my mother took a trip last year. I went to school here in Berkeley, and my sophomore year I went to school in Moraga. I did not like it there; I was suffocating there. In the Berkeley public schools there are the Spanish, there are the Blacks, there are the Asians, there is everything. So, I came back to El Cerrito High. After that, I went to Diablo Valley College and then transferred to UC Berkeley my junior year. I want to go to medical school. I would really like to stay here in the Bay Area. I am more American than Persian; I don't think I could really live back in Iran. I took a *Farsi* course last year, and they showed films of the [Persian] Empire. I have become interested in the art and architecture of Iran. I would like to go and see the ruins in Iran.

Ms. E ✄ One thing that I think is really important is that I know a lot of people who come here from Iran, like maybe three years ago, and have lived here only three or four years. They try to be all-American, and they just completely forget about their culture, about who they are and everything. I don't agree with that. I myself have grown up here for many years, and I am more Americanized than I am Persian. But I still like the music, I still like to associate myself, go to Persian gatherings with my family, or go to a Persian concert and still have fun and enjoy the music; and also I have my American friends, and so I am like both. I did not lose my identity as to who I am and no matter what you do, you can't really change who you are. I know a lot of people who come here and completely change. They don't like to speak *Farsi*. I have friends who say, "I don't speak it at my house. If I have to with my parents, I can't stand it."

Ms. B ✄ I have a problem with what you say because sometimes you might lose it, and it is not always intentional. Like for myself, when we moved over here, we did not have any extended family around us, and at the same time none of us in the family knew how to speak English. So, we started to speak English as a means of learning it, because none of us knew how to speak it, and it was more for practice to learn the language, and that turned into habit. So, in the family we only spoke English after a while. It was not that none of us wanted to speak *Farsi* because we had an aversion to speaking *Farsi*. It became a part of our life to speak English in the home, and because of that, I never really learned the language. Other people might look at me and say that oh, she wants not to be Persian, she wants to forget that she is Persian. It is not that at all. It is just that I did not grow up speaking it, and it was not a rebellion against being Persian. It just didn't happen, and other people might look at me and judge me because of that, and that pisses me off.

Mr. F ✂ *Is that bothersome or is it not? When people judge you, i.e., saying who is Persian and who is not. Let us say, in this case, because of language?*

Ms. E ✂ I am not necessarily just talking about the language. My parents speak *Farsi* at home because their English is not that good, although they have been here many years. But they still wanted me to know my language. So, they always spoke to me in *Farsi*. We speak only *Farsi* at home. I am just saying it really has to do with everything . . .

Ms. B ✂ You always had more extended family around you.

Ms. E ✂ Not really, not really, because, like I said, the majority of our family is back in Iran, and when we lived in London we did not have anybody in London, we did not have anybody in Canada either. My parents had a lot of Persian friends with whom they associated but that is about it. And most of our family is in Los Angeles.

Ms. B ✂ Your parents still have a lot of Persian friends like you said.

Ms. E ✂ My parents, yes.

Ms. B ✂ Not me, I did not have the tools to learn.

Ms. A ✂ You are talking about two different things. You are saying that your parents did not speak *Farsi* by choice, and you did not really have a choice because you were trying to learn English. I don't speak *Farsi* really, I was not raised with it. I speak very little and my father spoke it very little to us. But it wasn't because he did not want to teach me. He also wanted to practice English at home. Mainly it was because when my parents spoke to my brother, he was not responding to them in English, and they thought something was wrong with him. But then they realized that he responded in Spanish, and that was because the woman helping to take care of him spoke to him in Spanish. So, my dad really got scared that he could not communicate with his son. He only wanted to talk to him in English. From then on, we all just talked in English. That is why I don't speak *Farsi*. But it is really frustrating, and I think it is really unfair in a way to be treated as less of a Persian, or not as patriotic, or to have an inferior culture, or to hear comments that your dad did not raise you right. All four of us laugh at it. We can't deal with it any other way. It is clearly frustrating. It happens all the time. Even when I was in Greece this past summer, and this lady heard my name, a very Persian name. I was waiting, here it comes, here it comes, boom she starts speaking in *Farsi*, and now here comes the lecture. As soon as she found out that I don't speak *Farsi* she started, "Ah, you are Persian, it must be your dad who is Persian because your mom would teach you Persian because she would love the language," and on and on.

Mr. F ✂ *That is interesting. So if your mom was Persian, then she would have taught you, she would have talked to you.*

Ms. A ✎ That is what they say, but that is not true. They say that a lot, "Oh, your dad is Persian, well then, that makes sense." I am very proud of my Iranian heritage. I am concerned about the culture because my dad is . . . But I do agree that I am missing out on a whole lot by not speaking the language fluently, and I can't have as much of the culture as I like because language is a huge part of the culture. So, I am going to take *Farsi* next year. I really want to learn it. But in the meantime, you often get condemned. My sister took a lot of *Farsi* classes, and she speaks really well. She gets treated better by other Persians. It will never stop being frustrating, but I have learned how to endure it. I sit there with my brother and sister and think that here it comes, here it comes, the lecture and then boom there is the lecture: "You guys are Persians. How dare you not speak *Farsi*!"

Mr. F ✎ *How many kids in your family?*

Ms. A ✎ Four, I am the youngest.

Mr. F ✎ *How old is the oldest?*

Ms. A ✎ Twenty-five and I am twenty. And then they say, "Oh, your older sister speaks it because she is older in age." No, it is because she took *Farsi* classes. There are also two of my cousins, they speak very little *Farsi*. But maybe because they don't look as Persian or are not around as many Persians, they don't get as bad a treatment.

Ms. B ✎ It is really frustrating, it is difficult, it is offensive. When you don't know the situation, don't assume that I rebelled against it, or wasn't brought up right or . . .

Ms. A ✎ But even then, just the fact that I am proud to say that I am half-Persian and to have someone say . . .

Ms. B ✄ I never tell people that I am NOT Persian, but some people think I am Italian. I am not trying to pass off as an Italian or anything else, it is who I am. What you are interested in has a lot to do
with what you have been brought up with. So, I don't take as much
interest in Persian music. There are some that I like, the more traditional stuff that sounds familiar to me from my time when I was in
Iran. But it is not my favorite style of music, you know what I mean.
It is hard. That is why when I went to Berkeley I started taking *Farsi*
classes. I thought I am sick of this, I am going to learn it.

Ms. A ✄ My dad is really sympathetic with that. He says, "Don't
worry, don't listen to it." I think he feels bad because he knows what
we have to endure all the time.

Ms. B ✄ But this happens all the time . . .

Mr. F ✄ *What is good about America?*

Ms. B ✄ The diversity. The diversity of people, places, issues,
things. I like that a lot. It is hard for me to compare America with Iran
because I have not been to Iran for so long. But what I like about America is the diversity. I can't even say that about all of America; it is the
Bay Area. I like that, there is more flavor. After I had been in school
here in Berkeley, I went to school in Moraga for a year. When I would
go to my classes, I just kept saying to myself, where are all the people? because almost everybody was the same. I did not like it there at
all. I came back to Berkeley and went to high school around here.

Ms. A ✄ I also like the diversity, I like the opportunity, although I
don't think there is equal opportunity at all, but at least there is opportunity. I think Iran is more repressive, but I don't want to go on
about how repressive the government might be or condemn it.

Ms. E ✄ I agree with both of them. Iran has changed now ever since the time of the revolution about covering your hair, this and that. I think all that is a little too much. Here in America there is so much freedom, which I think is good, but sometimes there is too much freedom. There are a lot of crazy things out here; I think things should be balanced.

Mr. F ✄ *How about political freedom?*

Ms. A ✄ I don't think there is enough freedom.

Ms. B ✄ Freedom is wonderful. I mean it is good but with a little bit of self-discipline it is fine, allows for more creativity. There is just a lot of flavor here.

Ms. E ✄ I would rather have more freedom than having to cover my hair and not show my legs or arms in the dead of the sun and hot weather, but I think too much freedom can lead to a lot also.

Mr. F ✄ *Have you been bothered in America because of being an Iranian?*

Ms. B ✄ I can think of a very specific situation during the revolution, during the hostage crisis. I was probably in third grade, and I remember from that time. I was at a school here in Berkeley and a couple, well, a few kids took me into an alleyway and started hitting me, slapping me, and threatening me. They were girls. Finally a boy came and rescued me. I dealt with a lot of things during that time. It was in Washington School here in Berkeley. During the hostage crisis period, I dealt with a lot of flack. I remember during that time my parents owned a restaurant on Solano [Street]. There was a lot of vandalism of the restaurant, of the car. I just took a lot heat at the school. But that all stopped after the hostage crisis was over and things were normal, and I did not have to deal with anything again. Once in a while you hear terrorist remarks. But that is it.

Ms. E ⚞ I heard remarks here and there, but I really did not have anything happen to me. But I came to the States in 1986 or 1987.

Ms. A ⚞ I was in second or third grade, and the same situation happened, and stuff like that. This guy yelled and swore at me and told me to get off this playground. He called me an "IRANIAN" [pronounced eye-ranian]. I thought that is kind of weird, I just won't play in this playground. I did not really think anything of it. But I never wanted to hide it, I am totally Iranian. People's ignorance . . . you can always laugh at it. It is kind of scary, like people's ignorance when we were bombing Iraq and even the relation now with Iraq. Whenever I would express my sentiments, they would say, "Of course, you are from Iran." I would say, wait a second we just bombed Iraq, not Iran, get the difference between Iraq and Iran straight. But people don't really differentiate; if you are from the Middle East, that is it. If you are not white, you are it. There were a lot of hate crimes going on against Persians, not just Iraqis, when we were bombing Iraq. My mom was nervous because my dad's license plate says *azizam* ["my dear"]. She thought maybe someone was going to do something to him. Because people are so ignorant they can't tell the difference. I was also worried. I heard it on the radio, people looking in the phone book, and if the name look[ed] Iraqi or Iranian they would call up and repeatedly threaten them. What a joke all of this is. They never called our number. But I heard on the radio the stories and incidents happening to people whether they were Iraqi or not. Just hate crimes in general. What was that situation I am thinking of . . . well anyhow, nothing really against me besides once when I was little, the situation in the playground. I sort of thought it is amazing. I am more proud to be Iranian now. Now that it is like this, I will be more proud.

Mr. F ✕ *What about multiple identities and the transnational experience, being Iranian, American, and also something else? How do you experience this background or backdrop?*

Ms. A ✕ I am of mixed racial descent. I have dark skin and dark brown hair, but no distinguishing features that many people can identify. People don't know what I am, and I feel their uneasiness until their curiosity is appeased and the veil of tension is lifted. With each new job I begin, employees do not know how to relate to me until they know my racial heritage. I am not as threatening to them because I am mixed; my skin is not dark enough to do that. I sense the confusion among the employees until one of them gathers up the courage to ask the question they have all been dying to ask: "What are you?" Years of exposure to this form of ignorance has unfortunately led to my own confusion as to my cultural identity. However, my conversations with other mixed Persians revealed that I was not alone in my uncertainty. They too see blur where they should see an identity. For example, when I am Latina, I am only Latina, and when I am Persian, I am only allowed to be Persian. To Latinas, I look "undoubtedly" Latina, and to the Persians, I look "completely" Iranian. Therefore, even if I wanted to, it would not be possible for me to choose one identity over the other. It is very complicated to balance the two, as I am forced to perform the correct ethnic role with the appropriate group. It is difficult to maintain a double consciousness in a society that demands that I choose one. It is easier for people to relate to me as one or the other ethnicity, but not both. As a result, I am like a chameleon, changing from one identity to the next, constantly exercising extreme caution in order to prevent one part of me from acting inappropriately when I am expected to act like the other part of me. Or, in the more simple terms my friends use to describe me, I am "the Iran-Contra" girl.

SESSION 2

From a session with seven students—two women and five men—at the San Francisco Art Institute. My questions appear in italics.

Mr. Z ✖ I came here six years ago. I do not have much *ta'asub* [prej-udice] that I am an Iranian. I think of myself more as a Zoroastrian than an Iranian, because when we lived back in my own country we always had that *qorbat* [exile, longing] as a Zoroastrian. It was an Islamic country, and we, the Zoroastrians, felt like we were living in *qorbat*. When I came here, I did not feel any *qorbat*. I felt that I had more free-dom to be myself. I found the opportunity to get to know myself and to be away from issues and problems that come from *ta'asub*. The fact that my country is Iran, it is a *khak-o-abi* [land and water] to be pro-tected, does not have much value for me.

Mr. L ✖ I have been here sixteen years and when I came I was thir-teen years old. I also do not have any *ta'asub* that I am an Iranian, but until several years ago I thought of myself more as an Iranian because most of my life I had been in Iran. Now that I have been here more, I consider myself neither Iranian nor American. For me now, it is a sur-vival thing. If one does not have an attachment to one thing, it is be-cause tomorrow something else could happen for me not to be here. Once again, I must survive somewhere else.

Mr. F ✖ *Are your friends mostly American or Iranian?*

Mr. L ✖ Iranian.

Mr. F ✖ *And you have not forgotten Persian?*

Mr. L ✂ No. One reason was that a bunch of us lived in a small city. I lived for ten years in Fresno. I found a group of friends that had similar problems, we were Iranians the same age, we became very close together. The reason we became close together is that we could not relate to ordinary Iranians. By ordinary, I mean those who were more Iranian, who were still traditional. Also, fathers and mothers couldn't understand the problems that are here in this country. For this reason, we were of much help to each other.

Mr. K ✂ I grew up in Iran, and we left when I was eight and a half. My dad is Iranian and my mom is American. While we were there, among my friends, I was always considered Iranian even though my mom was American. It did not affect anyone's judgment of me as to who I was. The interesting thing is that when we came here during the hostage situation, it was similar in that it still did not matter if my mom was an American. I was needed as the scapegoat for a bunch of kids. Kids who really did not know what was going on, but who were reflecting what their parents were saying at home and listening to the racist attitudes that their parents did not want them really to hear, and yet they were anyway. I don't think that bumper stickers saying "Iranians Go Home" and different things in public helped their attitude any also. But, nevertheless, it affected mine. As far as my self-identity in Iran, I considered myself Iranian because that was all I ever knew. When I came here, at first I was proud to be Iranian. People would ask what is my name in Iranian and all that. It was a novelty having an Iranian in the class. As the hostage crisis continued, every-thing went reverse, and I was a scapegoat for lack of a better word. I lived in San Diego. Around where I grew up, there were a lot of surfers and a lot people who were into being native. Native Cali-fornian, native San Diegan, and anything that deviated from that norm was considered to be the "other." It is interesting the negative aspects taken on by the people and the countries that the U.S. has been in war with or had problems with. This happened with Iraq, too, and certain people here got a lot of trouble because of that.

Mr. F ✍ *You said that it would be nice for people to be able to live together, etc. I think about my father and mother's generation of people who have lived all their lives in Tabriz [a city in northwestern Iran]. In the manner that we see all types of communities and cultures here in San Francisco, they did not have or were not exposed to. The only other community that was there were the Armenians. The "other" were the Armenians, who had their own church, food, restaurants, liquor stores, good sandwiches, and silversmiths to the degree that I or we as Muslim children in Tabriz saw and were aware of the work and lives of Armenians. Or, for example, in the church or the community center, there were their dances, which were good. They used to celebrate Noel or Christmas, which was pretty and interesting. At any rate, here in San Francisco where we live today, an array of the world's peoples and cultures have been arranged for you to see.*

Ms. X ✍ Cosmopolitan!

Mr. F ✍ *Yeah, but I wonder to what extent? Maybe my expectations have gone too high. For example, I wonder what I have in common with a Vietnamese, or don't have for that matter? I go to their restaurants. Here, it is almost like human beings in a zoo. When viewed from a particular perspective, it is this collection of beautiful diversity and multiculturalism. But my feeling is that it has only stayed at the level of the restaurant.*

Ms. X ✍ The level of the restaurant! When you speak like this, one feels like a white American is talking. Please pardon me. When a person stands outside, one see all these foreigners, one is Vietnamese, the other is Chinese, the other is a Cambodian, and there is also Thai food that I should try. There are all of these. But the Vietnamese that you were speaking about are a good example, because when the Vietnam War took place I was in Iran. I was a kid, but it left a very weird effect on me. It raised the question of why is there a war in Vietnam? Why are the Americans doing all those things there? Why did the French go and do all those terrible things to those countries? That is how I look at the different people and nationalities that have come here.

Mr. Y ✄ When you go into a Vietnamese shop and confront a Vietnamese salesman today, that is not how you look at them, do you? You go in there, do your shopping, and come out. You don't think about all that has happened in Vietnam.

Ms. X ✄ That person has come out of that past and out of that history. One cannot forget that.

Mr. Y ✄ But one does, the problem is that one *does* forget. We in our daily lives do forget it. When you go into a 7-Eleven to buy something you don't take all that history with you in there. It is in our daily lives, in the daily encounters that we have—we must see what we do there. Some say that America is a melting pot. It is here that I agree with those who say it is not a melting pot but it is a salad bowl. There are different ingredients, but they have not mixed. They have not boiled together like a soup.

Ms. X ✄ Well, to an extent it has happened. For example, the marriage of different races together. Mr. K. is a good example of a melting pot. He is not an American, he is not an Iranian, he is both. Seriously, so when we say melting pot, one can talk about that, too, especially children who are from two different races. There are many of them, especially here in California.

Mr. Y ✄ You have Mr. K on one hand, and on the other, you have us which have not been assimilated into the pot yet. Or have not been melted into the other cheeses.

Mr. F ✂ *We have been and we have not, that is the whole point.*

Mr. Y ✂ That is the whole thing. You think you are, I think I am un-til I sit down and listen to some piece of music or something small hits me. It takes me some place where I cannot share it with other people around me who are not Iranian or don't have the same background. And it is painful sometimes not to be able to do that.

Ms. X ✂ Let us change the subject and go back a little. What I wanted to say is that I feel closer to many persons who come from the Third World. Let me say it this way. When an Iranian is disrespect-ful of a Mexican, I get angry. I tell them that we ourselves are Irani-ans, we live in this country under the burden of being foreigners.

Mr. H ✂ Let me point out something here. When I see you for the first time, I don't know whether you are Iranian or Spanish. Your face might look Spanish. My first encounter with you is a human one, in that I want to see what kind of person you are and what goes on in your head as a human. If it happens that you are one of my country-men, it is possible that we may have something in common. I don't agree with this, that I see the world like this because I am here in America and that America was not in agreement with my country. Many ordinary people have been born here, which happens to be America, and have started to live and work here.

Ms. X ✂ But they govern us with their laws.

Mr. H ✂ That is a different issue. As far as the subject of identity is concerned and on many issues, Americans are supportive of your ideas and position. In fact, as a foreigner, they support you.

Mr. K ✂ I have a problem with the melting pot allegory in that if we say that my Iranian half is a zucchini and my American half is a carrot and you throw them into the melting pot, gradually my carrot juices and my zucchini juices are going to be sucked out, and what is left is still a little piece of dehydrated zucchini and dehydrated carrot, and still exists no matter how much you try to boil it off. Because of that, first of all, I am neither an American nor Iranian. Second of all, I am an Iranian and I am an American, but the juices have been taken out of me, in that I have lost my language partially because my dad never spoke [it] to me, partially because it was socially unacceptable to be speaking it with friends in elementary school. My American side has been taken out of me with Reagan and Bush funding both sides of the Iran and Iraq war. And I can't even love my American side and I cannot love my Iranian side. Therefore, have I been melted into an American? I don't think so.

Mr. F ✕ One quick point. Nowadays there is a lot of discussion about the unmeltables, which is, I think, the salad analogy that you are saying.

Mr. Y ✕ Yes. We realize that there are differences and there are different cultural entities. When we realize this, then we can have better relations between these cultural entities rather than believing that they are losing all their colors and juices into one product and into one shape. This is the double-edged nature of assimilation. America means that we would be dealing with each other in our most common denominators, whether you are from Vietnam, Iceland, Iran, or anywhere. You put us in one place [and] we have to, because of instincts for survival, find our most basic common denominators, which means that anything that is idiosyncratic in particular cultures is going to be wiped away, either immediately or gradually. The other side of the coin is that if you are to gain something out of this assimilation you have to lose something whether you want to or not. It is inevitable; you can't have both.

Mr. F ✂ *America is not static. They are really trying to figure out what is going on.*

Mr. Y ✂ Because these common denominators are shifting higher or lower, depending on which culture comes in and which one becomes more economically viable to deal with. Whether Koreans come up, Japanese come up, or the others come up.

Mr. F ✂ *Certainly in the next few decades this whole notion of multicultur-alism is going to be put to [the] test. I think there is a lot of lip service, now espe-cially here in California. One can distinctly feel that there is a lot of lip service from the government, the state, and institutions trying to diffuse some kind [of] energy and dynamism that is perceived not to be healthy. On the other hand, I think there is a process of ghettoization that is taking place in this period of mul-ticultural plurality in this country. My point is that, simultaneous with what ap-pears to be more involvement with the mainstream of American society, a process of isolation and segregation is taking place, especially for the older generation of Iranians or others who have come to this country in the past twenty or thirty years. The reasons for this among Iranians are both internal and external. One can see also that [in] other groups, different ethnic and cultural groups and communities are becoming an island unto themselves. They are developing cultural and eco-nomic resources, such as an ethnic economy, etc. But for the most part, meaningful interaction takes place or is supposed to take place with your own group or within one's own group. At least for Iranians, there is only superficial interaction with other groups, such as Euro/Anglo-Americans, but especially with non-Euro/Anglo-Americans, such as Afro-Americans, Native Americans, Chinese, Viet-namese, Koreans, Indians, and Hispanic/Latin Americans. This is what I meant by an arranged collection of beautiful diversity and multiculturalism, and that it has more or less stayed at the level of the restaurant.*

Authors' Biographies

REZA ASHRAH was born in Berkeley, California, to Iranian parents and is the second of three children. Having returned to Iran five times to date, Reza feels an intense connection to his Persian heritage; he feels, however, just as strongly attached to the United States. Growing up as a gay Iranian-American in the culturally diverse environment of the San Francisco Bay Area, Reza has found inspiration in both cultures. In addition to being a poet, Reza is also a pianist and vocalist and often uses his poems as song lyrics for his band, Taka.

PARINAZ ELEISH was born and raised in Iran and educated in the United States. She has an M.A. in film from Boston University and an M.A. in English from the University of New Hampshire. Her work has been published in several literary journals in the United States including *The International Quarterly, International Poetry Review*, and *The Literary Review*.

AZADEH FARAHMAND was born and raised in Tehran and emigrated to the United States in 1989 when she was sixteen years old. In her fourth year of undergraduate studies at UCLA's School of Engineering, she gave up science for philosophy; in the Department of Philosophy, she reclaimed her passion for the arts and the humanities. A poet since the age of thirteen, she writes poetry and prose in both Persian and English. Her work has appeared in *TERUA I, Persian Book Review*, and *Daftar-e Shenakht*. Farahmand recently obtained an M.A. in Cinema Studies from the school of Film and Television at UCLA, where she is pursuing a Ph.D. She is currently involved in numerous multimedia and documentary projects.

Tara Fatemi studied at the University of California at Santa Cruz and received an M.A. in poetry from the University of Texas at Austin in 1997. Her poems have been published in several journals, and she has been a featured speaker at poetry readings and conferences on both literature and the Middle East. She is very happy that her poems are appearing alongside the expressions of other Iranian-American writers and hopes that this collection will encourage further dialogue both inside and outside Iranian-American communities.

Zjaleh Hajibashi grew up in Lubbock, Texas. In addition to writing poetry and fiction, she has published articles on Persian literature and reviews of recent writing about the Middle East. She spent nearly two years in Iran after the revolution conducting research for her dissertation, *The Fiction of the Post-Revolutionary Iranian Woman*. While in Iran, Hajibashi was the editor of the English-language magazine, *Film International*, published in Tehran. She holds B.A. degrees in English Literature and Biological Science from Rice University, an M.A. in Persian Literature, and a Ph.D. in Comparative Literature from the University of Texas.

Zara Houshmand was born in the United States to an American mother and an Iranian father. She spent her childhood in the Philippines and received a B.A. in English from London University. Her award-winning translations of Bijan Mofid's plays and her own plays, *The Future Ain't What It Used to Be* and *In Xanadu*, have been produced in New York, Los Angeles, and San Francisco. She is the editor of several books on Buddhism and science and a pioneer in the development of virtual reality on the Internet.

Jahanshah Javid has been publishing *The Iranian* and *The Iranian Times* on the Internet since 1995 (www.iranian.com). Born in the oil town of Abadan, Iran, in 1962, Javid began a career in journalism in the early 1980s as a reporter for the Iranian News Agency (IRNA). During the early 1990s, he also freelanced for the BBC World Service's Persian Service and the Associated Press. From 1994 to 1996 he presented an Iranian cultural program on Aftab cable television in the United States. Javid holds a B.A. in media studies from Hunter College, City University of New York.

TARA KAI is the name the author chose for herself when she moved to Los Angeles from Germany. She was born in Tehran, spent her childhood in London, and received an M.A. in American Studies and Media Studies from Paderborn University in Germany. Her publications include the short stories "Room for a Refugee" and "If Only They Had Asked Me." She recently finished her first novel, Dar-Es-Salaam, and is currently working on a second novel. She lives in Santa Monica, California.

PERSIS M. KARIM was born to an Iranian father and a French mother and raised in the San Francisco Bay Area. She has long sought a home in one culture, and after numerous years of seeking and too many years of education, she has resigned herself to the fact that a piece of her lies in three continents, in three different cultures and languages. Karim holds a B.A. in Community Studies from the University of California at Santa Cruz, an M.A. in Middle Eastern Studies, and a Ph.D. in Comparative Literature from the University of Texas. In addition to writing fiction and poetry, she has written on contemporary Persian, French, and American literature dealing with experiences of exile, migration, and displacement. She currently lives in the Bay Area, teaches at the University of California at Santa Cruz, and hopes to visit Iran for the first time very soon.

FIROOZEH KASHANI-SABET received a Ph.D. in history from Yale University. Her book, Frontier Fictions: Shaping the Iranian Nation, 1804–1946, is forthcoming from Princeton University Press. She has completed the manuscript for a novel, entitled Hidden Faces of Parsa, from which her short story, "Martyrdom Street," has been excerpted. She lives in New Haven, Connecticut, where she promotes backgammon, Persian dancing, and vegetarianism—all with little success.

LALEH KHALILI was born in Philadelphia in 1968 and later moved to Iran, where she lived until 1985. At the age of seventeen, she moved to the United States and obtained a B.S. in chemical engineering from the University of Texas. After five years as a management consultant, she returned to academia. She is currently working on her master's degree in International Affairs at Columbia University.

NIKA KHANJANI moved from Isfahan to Houston with her parents in 1979. She is currently a senior at the University of Texas at Austin studying English Literature and Community Planning. Khanjani is a Baha'i, which, to a large extent, shapes her Iranian identity. She loves swing dancing and *sholeh-zard*.

Born and raised in Iran, MOHAMMAD MEHDI KHORRAMI left his country in 1982 for political reasons. He continued his education in France and the United States and received a Ph.D. from the University of Texas at Austin in 1996. He has published a number of articles on postrevolutionary Persian fiction and on the literature of exile. He is also the author of a number of short stories and two novels, *Sayehay-e Zendegi* (1986) and *Ketab-e Afarinesh* (1990), and is currently working on a screenplay about the life of Sadegh Hedayat. He lives in New York where he teaches Persian language and literature at New York University.

FARNOOSH MOSHIRI was born in Tehran. She received a B.A. in Dramatic Literature from the College of Dramatic Arts and an M.A. in Drama from the University of Iowa. Her plays, short stories, and poems were published in Iranian literary magazines before the revolution. Her first novel, *At the Wall of the Almighty*, will be published in the spring of 1999. Moshiri is currently working toward a Ph.D. in Creative Writing and Literature while preparing a collection of short stories and her second novel. She teaches literature and creative writing at the University of Houston.

SIAMAK NAMAZI is an Iranian-American living in Bethesda, Maryland. He holds an M.S. in Urban Planning from Rutgers University and a B.A. in International Relations from Tufts University. After completing his degree in 1993, he decided to return Iran to fulfill his mandatory military service. Namazi has lived and worked in Iran, the United States, Egypt, Kenya, and Somalia. He is currently Director of Future Alliances International, a strategic consulting firm focusing on the Middle East. He has written several articles on policy issues relating to Iran.

SANAZ NIKAEIN graduated from high school with honors at the age of sixteen and, at eighteen, was the youngest graduate ever from Diablo Valley College to receive an Associate Arts degree with honors. She currently studies at the University of California, Berkeley, and is pursuing a double major in Psychology and Near Eastern Studies. She plans to attend law school after graduation and hopes to publish a collection of her poetry before then. Nikaein credits all of her accomplishments to the love and support of her mother, Mahin, and of Samira, Ali, Homayoon, and the rest of her family.

MARYAM OVISSI is an artist and a poet. She has also pursued a professional career in the arts at such institutions as the Arthur M. Sackler Gallery, the Freer Gallery of Art, and the Museum of Fine Arts, Boston. She is currently at the Asian Art Museum in San Francisco. In 1998, Ovissi opened Gallery Ovissi in the San Francisco Bay Area; it is the first gallery in the United States dedicated to exhibiting the work of contemporary Iranian and Middle Eastern artists.

SAÏDEH PAKRAVAN is of Iranian origin (though descended from many other nationalities, including Austrian, Polish, Irish, Italian, and Dutch). She is French-educated and lives in the United States. A published writer of fiction, nonfiction, and poetry, she is also the editor in chief of an Iranian cross-cultural quarterly in English, *Chanteh*. A book of Pakravan's stories about Iran is soon to be released. She often gives readings in the Washington, D.C., area, where she lives with her family.

NAHID RACHLIN was born in Iran and came to the United States to attend college. She married an American and stayed on. Since moving to this country she has been writing and publishing novels and short stories in English. Among her publications are three novels, *Foreigner, Married to a Stranger,* and *The Heart's Desire,* and a collection of short stories, *Veils.* Rachlin's stories have been published in many magazines. As a student, she held a Doubleday-Columbia fellowship and a Wallace Stegner Fellowship. Among the grants and awards she has received are the Bennet Cerf Award, PEN Syndicated Fiction Project Award, and a grant from the National Endowment for the Arts. She currently teaches creative writing at the New School for Social Research, New York.

DONNÉ RAFFAT is the author of *The Caspian Circle, The Prison Papers of Bozorg Alavi,* and *The Folly of Speaking,* a novel soon to be published. He has reviewed for *The Los Angeles Times, The New York Times,* and *The Nation.* Raffat teaches English and Comparative Literature at San Diego State University.

NASRIN RAHIMIEH was born in Bandar Anzali, Iran. She has lived in the United States, Switzerland, and Canada, where she completed her education. She now lives in Edmonton with her husband and four cats and teaches Comparative Literature at the University of Alberta. Rahimieh's academic work concerns Iranian experiences of exile. Her most recent work includes *Missing Persians,* a book-length study of Persian transculturation, and an English translation of *The Virgin of Solitude,* the late Taghi Modarressi's last novel.

ARASH SAEDINIA was born in Iran and raised in Los Angeles. He received a B.A. in Political Science and Peace and Conflict Studies from the University of California, Berkeley, in 1995. Saedinia spent the following two years teaching in Southern California's inner cities, raising a pug named "Meshky," and completing a master's degree in English. Currently a student at Harvard Law School, Saedinia divides his time between coasts and enthusiasms. His grandparents, Bibi and Sharif, are in their nineties.

FEREYDOUN SAFIZADEH received an undergraduate degree in Social Relations and a Ph.D. in Anthropology and Middle Eastern Studies from Harvard University. He has taught anthropology at Harvard University, Amherst College, Boston University, UCLA, and San Francisco State University. His interests include anthropology of the Middle East and the Caucasus, ethnicity and identity, and visual anthropology. At present he is a visiting scholar at the Center for Middle Eastern Studies at Harvard University doing research on issues of identity in the Republic of Azerbaijan.

MARIAM SALARI was born in Cleveland, Ohio, in 1974. She grew up in Lakeland, Florida, with her parents and two brothers, Ali and Amir. After receiving a B.A. in English from Tulane University, Salari spent a year doing volunteer work for Habitat for Humanity in Louisiana. She later moved to New York City and obtained an M.A. from Columbia University. She still lives in New York City and plans to obtain her doctorate from Columbia University in Communications while teaching.

SOLMAZ SHARIF wrote her poem "My Father's Shoes" when she was thirteen. Her parents were active participants in the Iranian Revolution and left Iran before Sharif was born (in Istanbul, Turkey). She came to the United States with her parents when she was fifty days old. Until the winter of 1997, Sharif had never been to Iran. During her visit there, she was impressed by its rich history and culture and especially enjoyed the city of Isfahan and its beautiful architecture. Sharif currently attends high school in Los Angeles, California.

Reza Shirazi was born and raised in Bombay, India; his parents are of Iranian origin. He received his B.S. in Business and English Literature from the University of Kansas and his M.B.A. from the University of Texas at Austin. Shirazi lives and works in Austin, Texas. His poems have been published in the *Texas Observer, Coal City Review, Midwest Poetry Review, Parnassus, Potato Eyes,* and *The Space Between Our Footsteps: Poems and Paintings from the Middle East.*

Nazanin Sioshansi was born in Tehran and emigrated to the United States in 1979, eight months after the revolution. She grew up in Lincoln, Massachusetts, and received a B.A. in English from Middlebury College. She is currently working at the Advisory Board Company in Washington, D.C., and plans to attend business school in the year 2000.

Sassan Tabatabai was born in Tehran and has lived in the United States, along with his family, since 1980. He is currently a Ph.D. candidate at the University Professors Program, Boston University, where he is working on an annotated English translation of the collected poems of Rudaki, a tenth-century Iranian poet. His essays, poems, and translations have appeared in numerous publications including *The Christian Science Monitor, Comment,* and *The Republic of Letters.*

Ramin M. Tabib is a resident of Los Angeles and works as a research analyst for a Japanese firm. He was born in Iran in 1966 and left when he was seventeen. Tabib holds a B.S. in Engineering and an M.A. and A.B.D. in Political Science from the University of Southern California. He is a frequent contributor to the on-line magazine *The Iranian* and hopes to publish his first novel some time before the great asteroid hits the earth.

Roxanne Varzi was born to an American mother and an Iranian father in Tehran in 1971. After receiving a B.A. in conflict resolution and Middle East Studies from the American University in Washington,

D.C., Varzi returned to Iran for a year. "The Pelican" is an excerpt from her book, *Majnun's Mask*, about her year there. In it, she deals with the boundaries of identity, fiction and nonfiction, and memory and reality. A Ph.D. student in Anthropology at Columbia University, Varzi focuses on issues of identity and spatial representation in post-revolutionary Iranian cinema and literature.

MICHAEL C. WALKER is a writer, scholar, and researcher who has long been interested in Iran from both an historical perspective and a perspective of personal heritage. Walker is best known for his contributions to the fields of epidemiology and public health and has published research on the status of medicine in developing and war-torn regions. Following the example set by such writers as Susan Sontag and Paul Goodman, Walker tries not to limit his writing to one area, but instead considers any field that he finds interesting and of social or cultural import.

KATAYOON ZANDVAKILI was born in Tehran and raised in the United States. She holds a B.A. in Social Sciences from the University of California at Berkeley and an M.F.A. from Sarah Lawrence College, New York. Her book, *Deer Table Legs*, was awarded the University of Georgia's Contemporary Poetry Prize and was released by the university's press in 1998. A West Coast Associate for *Publishers Weekly*, Zandvakili lives in the San Francisco Bay Area and is currently working on a novel.

ALI ZARRIN was born in Kermanshah, Iran, in 1952 and emigrated to the United States in 1970. He received a B.A. in English from the University of Colorado at Boulder, an M.A. in English Literature from the University of Colorado at Denver, and a Ph.D. in Comparative Literature from the University of Washington at Seattle. Zarrin has published four books of verse in Persian and four in English. He is also the author of *The Interplay of Self & Other in Selected Iranian Short Stories, 1906–1979*. Zarrin is the poetry editor of *Interpoetics*, an on-line literary magazine; he also teaches at a number of colleges and universities throughout the United States.

SHADI ZIAEI was born in Tehran in 1969 and moved to the United States in 1986. She received a B.A. in Creative Writing from San Francisco State University and is currently working on a collection of poems. "Death Observed" is dedicated to Anthony Julian Wright, whose passion for art and architecture inspires her.